The Curmudgeon

The Curmudgeon

A novel by

J. Hayes Hurley

Publisher is Croesus Books

ISBN 978-1-257-64536-7

To John Dufour

Cover Art: "Squaring the Circle"

Douglas Leichter

One

My name is Martin Parrish, but call me Marty. I'm writing this in San Francisco where I live in the same rambling top story apartment on Nob Hill I did as a child. My parents passed away in the early sixties leaving me sole title to this property. My older sister was happy with the arrangement; she was already married, had moved to the East coast, and more importantly, ended up inheriting the cash from the family estate.

At the time, I was a first-year assistant professor of philosophy at San Francisco State. I say philosophy because that was the department I was assigned to, but in fact, I am a logician with strong ties to foundational mathematics. I was married in 1966 at the age of thirty to a young woman twelve years my junior who voluntarily dropped out of her freshman year of college in order to accommodate me. She was someone I had high hopes for; I meant to train her mind privately although that never worked out. We had five children together: two boys and three girls. Every one of them has moved out of this place now, including my no-good, soon to be ex-wife, leaving me all alone again in this grand apartment. Four of my children still live in the city. I have weekly contact with them; another daughter and I keep in contact through e-mail. My no-good, soon to be ex-wife has relocated to Miami Beach and formed the habit of only calling when she wants money, which is quite often.

Though I have a deep love for my city and carry a fierce loyalty to the Nob Hill neighborhood, never once have I been caught up in any of the ideological waves that periodically pass through—be they homegrown or imported. As well, I have avoided publicly digging in my heels in opposition to any of these movements, though more often than not I find them without sense. I cannot say the same for my soon to be ex-wife, my five kids, or most of the residents of San Francisco. I am blessed with a natural immunity to sociological diseases of consciousness, being able to distinguish between thoughts and concepts—though my children have it that I am an embittered old fart. They also accuse me of being a right-winger, but in that, they are wrong. I am a liberal. It's just that I'm a quiet liberal and not given to activism, advocacy, or marching. Let me explain.

Right after I got married, the flower children invaded this city. They flooded then eventually overwhelmed the California welfare rolls. They said they were trying to break the system but that was a lie; they wanted to live for free while they smoked their dope. I met hundreds of them and visited a number of their so-called communes over near Golden Gate Park, doing so for educational purposes only. As many as forty young people would arrive by Greyhound bus and spread sleeping bags out on the floor of an apartment a third the size of mine. They would smoke marijuana from the time they woke up until the time they went to sleep. They collected their welfare checks and their food stamps with religious fervor, survived on frozen ice cream pies and chocolate chip cookies and, thanks to their practice of free-love spread gonorrhea like it was a hot political rumor. But here's the deal: I never dropped a dime on any of them. I disapproved of what they did but I was passively tolerant. That's why I can say I am a liberal. I acted exactly the same way towards rednecks who came here from places like Idaho to make trouble, though no one noticed my restraint.

This is San Francisco. We are mostly an affluent population and culturally on the cutting edge. Since I'm a quiet liberal, I'm terribly misunderstood. I can take it. I can take just about anything except further calls from my no-good, soon to be ex-wife. My home is on Clay Street just off the corner of Taylor. From my living room window, I gaze out diagonally at the V-J Grocery Store with its old-fashioned sign advertising liquor and fresh sandwiches. The store opened right after World War II. I am seventy-two years old so I was there to hail its opening and cheer its patriotic fervor. I have been doing light shopping there since I was nine. I would say my values are V-J values and there is nothing wrong with that; one can be both patriotic and a liberal. I never went around town trying to explain this because, invariably, I would've been branded a conservative.

Silent in public, I did try my best in my own household. My kids wouldn't listen to me and still won't. My wife never appreciated the guidance I offered or my forgiveness of her inadequacies. The greatest disappointment in my life, one that visits me over and over again, is the fact that no one in my household took advantage of the training I provided them in logical argumentation. My children referred to me as Genghis Kahn while I was raising them and, now that I am old, they call me a curmudgeon.

It's a bad rap. I see things as they transpire. I refuse to fall into false consciousness while my wife and children run headlong into that trap every time. Rather, I see what's to be seen without straining it through some ideological lens. For instance, when people started moving into shaky neighborhoods around this city a few years ago, I said, okay, put your money down and take a chance, nothing wrong with that. But that was not good enough for my wife. She would yell at me:

"Marty, you are so *negative*."

Why was I being negative? The neighborhoods were not much to look at and, even now that they have renovated the houses and the new owners have gotten themselves mortgaged to the hilt they *still* are not the sorts of places any right-minded person would care to live in. I am *not* negative. I am realistic and, as I said, quietly tolerant. Frankly, I do not feel the need or see the point of going around declaring my enthusiasm for something that's a lukewarm undertaking at best. People could have done better putting their money into bonds yet I never thought of interfering.

Now that I am alone and retired from teaching I want to tell my story in hope that there are readers out there that might read it without losing their tempers and tossing the book against the wall, though I have few allusions. Before she left me to go to Miami Beach to sell real estate in a South Beach market that was already collapsing, my wife used to throw into the garbage can any copies of *The Wall Street Journal* I brought home. She would scream out,

"We only read two papers in this household, *The San Francisco Chronicle* and *The New York Times*.

I would patiently explain to her that I read those papers, too, and was only trying to get balance. "Sophia! We ought search everywhere for that little bit of news that isn't tainted when they tear down the firewall between editorial and front page. To do that we do better when we filter our way through both sides even while knowing that both sides are tainted."

"I *won't* have that right wing paper in my house!"

We battled for years over that particular subject.

Sophia eventually won the war by taking the fight too far. She started pasting articles from the Times Style Section on Modern Love on our refrigerator. There was one I remember where a woman, writing in the first person as they all do, described in detail the inadequacies of her third husband's penis, comparing it to several of her younger lovers ever-standing equipment, and how she had to comfort him while simultaneously breaking various glass ceilings, meanwhile retaining the best divorce lawyers on the side just in case and while not missing a single summer weekend in the Hamptons where she would run into her first ex-husband's second wife and compare notes with her about care giving and charitable events, returning to Manhattan on Sunday nights to have supper with her ancient father who had, when the author was four years old, abused her according to memories supplied by her psychoanalyst, with whom she was having an affair, but only so that she could research her book, tentatively titled "I".

Two

This is a city made for walking so long as you can handle the hills. I walk every day. It does pain me to see eighty-year old Chinese ladies heading up the same hill I am heading down. Their steps are so tiny and their movements so slow I am reminded of that Wittgensteinian puzzler about whether or not the old man is going up or down the mountain. I am having a bit of trouble with hills these days myself. For the first time in my life I will admit to skirting one or two of the steeper ones on my daily walks.

I *do* love my city and I am perhaps the only resident who speaks without prejudice or ideological bent, so I have always kept silence regarding its so-called beauty. True enough, if you are crossing certain intersections where the hills on either side of you plunge down to the water's edge it can take your breath away, but not every street corner offers these views. On the contrary San Francisco is filled with turn of the century houses that in all honesty are ugly to look at. Many of them are painted that blue-grey color that is supposed to mimic the water, the fog, and the spirit of this city, but instead only promote and then promulgate a certain dreariness that, whenever I pointed this out to my wife, would trigger the same old response.

"You pulled me out of college and married me so as to fill my head with your bias. I won't listen anymore."

"You never *did* listen, Sophia! I am not knocking San Francisco architecture per se. I am only saying that some buildings are worthy of praise while large numbers of them are not."

"You are so negative."

"I am being objective!"

"Negative!"

I should have let Sophia stay in school and study English literature. I certainly couldn't get her to expand her vocabulary. That is the rub: people fail to be experts, fail to develop, fail to understand, fail to see things as they really are, yet their egos go on operating like a bunch of squirrels trying to bite and claw their way into your attic. To be alive and uninformed; to be alive and flat out wrong; to be alive and uninformed and flat out wrong and yet ever willing to shove one's opinions down someone else's throat, why, that makes this a frustrating world.

The first two years of our marriage were not all that bad. Sophia was willing to listen to me at times and she did take some of my advice. It made her a better person even though she threw all of it back into my face later.

"You never let me breathe, Marty. You never let me grow."

Yes, well, it was me who kept scatterbrained, teenage Sophia out of communes and off dope. I was me who let her run wild in department stores buying enough clothes to outfit a small community. Meanwhile I was the one who suffered silently when she told me she would rather eat glass than to sit around the dining room table nights listening to me explain truth tables.

Anyway we *were* mostly happy. We used to go to V-J Saturday mornings, get supplies for a picnic, walk down to the water, talk, laugh, kiss; I will never forget those days and Sophia's divorce lawyers can't make me.

Our first child, Jason, was born in 1970. I cannot tell you how happy we were, Sophia and I, to be parents. Jason was a big, strapping baby and was, as I was soon to find out to my delight, as bright as they come in human form. Whatever intellectual failings I discovered in Sophia would be more than made up for, I thought, now that Jason was on board.

Jason is a common name for boys these days. Not so back in 1970. I named him after Jason the Argonaut, not being unmindful of the fact that the term Argonaut was used to describe those who took part in the California gold rush of 1849. Jason was our golden nugget.

As soon as he learned to read I took over his philosophical training. I had it in mind to educate my son the way James Mill did his son John Stuart, though with this difference: Jason would grow up robust and lusty as well as logical and subtle. He would suffer no depressions and he certainly would be a man's man. Sophia objected to my supplementing our son's public schooling with my private tutoring but she quickly relented. It finally entered her head that if I was training Jason she was off the hook.

I did not require that Jason read Greek and Latin classics. I made the judgment that our educational system had passed beyond that. What I did do was start my boy in on baby logic when he was five years old and I pressed on from there so that when he entered the prestigious prep school we got him into armed with my checkbook he was, in my mind, already prepared to write articles for the Journal of Symbolic Logic, a publication that looked favorably upon me throughout my career, albeit not that often.

As far as thinkers went, I turned Jason onto the early British Analysts and encouraged him to supplement his logical studies with the ordinary language efforts of G. E. Moore. I wanted Jason to be able to attack a problem either logically or linguistically with equal skill. As for results, the boy exceeded my wildest hopes; when he was sixteen he was both captain of his lacrosse team and able to critique the papers *I* was writing in order to secure my tenure. Sophia never gave me her blessing for working with Jason though she did hold her tongue seeing that the boy blossomed; we both loved Jason dearly.

Jason went to Princeton. I took some credit for that. He continued to be an athlete and a scholar and his luck with the ladies was such that after his freshman year he did not come home summers to be with us but was off to tony places with this socially connected beauty or that. Sophia would cry but I was delighted. I wanted Jason to do his doctorate in philosophical logic back east in an Ivy League setting and I had visions of our family establishing a bicoastal presence.

Three

Jason used his systematic logical training all right. He did so to open a chain of hardware stores all over this city. He is now adding a second franchise venture; he is moving into pluming supplies. He is even talking down the line about a third chain, this one involving sporting goods.

Jason's adult life, his business interests, his conversations, his dreams and hopes and aspirations bore me to tears. Worse, Jason thinks I ought to be enthused about how he has turned out and about his values and his business success. I am not. We have been battling ever since he returned from college in 1992 to open his first store and we continue sniping at one another today. Frankly, Jason's business interests have nothing to do with my anti-ideological stances and everything to do with my idiosyncratic nature; I just cannot stand being in hardware stores. I cannot stand the very idea of uniformity. It drives me mad. Let me expound.

When he started in business I went into one of Jason's stores to see him. He gave me a nod to let me know he would be right with me, but first he had to finish helping a customer select the right screw. Do you have any idea how many different kinds of screws there are in this one world? There are millions of screw types! Suffice to say it takes an eternity to complete a single transaction, and Jason, like many of his customers, enjoys the inanity. The details never stop coming; every thread and turn and head has to be discussed, mulled over, and *felt*.

Some customers who had already made their purchases wouldn't leave. They stayed there in the aisle reveling in talk about drills or hammers or awls or the like. I went mad. Jason took issue with my impatience.

"Dad! What is *wrong* with you? Screws are fascinating. Without screws where would the world be?"

"Jason! Without screws there would have been no need for Karl Marx. We would, all of us, have escaped alienation, the worst forms of the division of labor, the excesses of capitalism, the polarization of private property, and the cookie-cutter civilization we suffer today. It was the industrial age that screwed us if you will forgive the pun."

"Oh, Dad. What are you on about now? Marx has been in the ground for a century and a half. San Francisco is part of the real world. We need hardware and we need to know that the screws we buy fit, that they are well built, and that they can be replaced as needed. Somebody has to guarantee that. I am that guarantee."

"Your life is a bore."

"No, Dad. You are wrong. You are the one with the problem. You are impatient, intolerant pigheaded, opinionated, and I don't know what else, but give me time and I'll think of it."

The most disappointing thing for me was that Jason was able to turn the tables and blame my critique of his life on my personality shortcomings. I had cautioned my son not to give into the temptation of employing the genetic fallacy, yet every time I complained about his turning his life over to screws and such, he went right ahead and did so. I *am* an impatient man but what does that have to do with the greater issue?

Sometimes, it is true, Jason counter-argued effectively, like when I railed against the big supermarket chains muscling into the bay area and touted the V-J Grocery Store as my ideal my son returned a vivid description of how many trucks it would take to supply a vast network of tiny, family owned grocery stores and how those trucks would tie up traffic and cause distribution nightmares such that the sheer redundancy of it all would sent prices skyrocketing.

"Be fair, Dad. You have the luxury of being an elitist. You can afford to stroll a few feet over to V-J one day, and go out to dinner the next. For most folks a week without the big supermarkets would be a disaster."

"Well … yes, but …"

"What?"

"If you can argue so well why are you not in academia?"

"Oh, Dad."

My point was that Jason used his training to open businesses. I found that a waste of intelligence and still do. Does that make me an elitist? That very concept, elitism, is ideologically tainted to begin with: brand someone with elitism and all you are doing is promoting your own cause.

Jason's move into plumbing supplies happened starting in 2002. If I thought I was as bored as one could be being in his hardware stores I was wrong; watching him help a customer find the right lip to fasten onto a length of pipe, a search that involved dragging out a half-dozen manuals, three different computer programs, and, to top it all, engaging in a frank forty-five minute conversation about how they used to make that part but discontinued it and how we might be able to get around the problem by substituting another kind of part but how that would entail some labor which brings in cost factors unless you can do the work yourself, would take me from mere madness on into sheer hell. I yelled at Jason one day,

"Imagine the knights of old out in search of a lip to fit onto a pipe to connect up to a toilet instead of the Holy Grail?

"Oh, yeah! What sort of a life do you think we would have here in the city without uniform plumbing supplies? Huh? I will tell you. The streets of San Francisco would be piled up with shit!"

"Don't get vulgar with me young man."

"Dad, you drive me to it."

Jason would go on and on about the necessity of having uniform supplies in order to build sewage systems and the like and we would both get talking about the Romans and their houses, speculating as to whether or not they had uniformity when neither one of us had a clue. Now and again my son tried to gain some distance, crying out,

"Dad, Dad, why are we fighting?"

I would fire back:

"It is because you can't see the humor in it."

"Me? Me?"

"Jason, I will not get into father-son Freudian entanglements when the truth of the matter is that *you* can't see the philosophical side of screws and nuts and bolts and stuff."

At this point Sophia would step in to defend our son against me.

"Marty! Your son is a runaway success. He made more money this year than you did after decades of teaching your damn courses. Why don't you acknowledge him? Why don't you congratulate him? Why do you have to be so difficult? So he is not an academic like you. So what? Better still … thank God!"

I did not and do not begrudge Jason his financial success. That was never the point. The point is that he wasted his mind. He has a good mind and it is well trained. A mind that good and that well trained ought not be rummaging around in hardware or plumbing supplies. Jason always argued that plumbing supplies were a natural outgrowth from hardware per se and I grant that, but what about this latest thing, sporting equipment? How does that follow?

"Dad, I used to play lacrosse, right? I can see what is needed in any sport and I know how to supply it. Once more, I know how to compete. A thousand guys get into sporting goods and only a few make it. I will make it and I will drive my competition out. I am a crackerjack businessman. At least give me that."

"I am *not* denying that you are a crackerjack businessman, Jason. Make all the money you want! Just don't go around behind my back like your mother does saying I am jealous. It is just … Jason. Tell me something. How can you stand it? A customer comes into one of your stores asking for a can of paint. You show him a dozen kinds of paint. Satin finish, semi-gloss, high gloss, oil-based, water-base, acrylic base, or what have you. That is … Jason. The idea of your being philosophically trained at home was for you to appreciate the oneness of reality, not to get into its details so that … so that everything begins and ends in details."

"Dad, I will give you a pass. You are … I will tell you what you are. You are disgruntled. You are a disgruntled old man. You are a *character*. You are always talking about how, once a person has his logical training down, he would acquire this vision of the whole, but then you undercut that by trashing every thinker who came before Russell. *I* remember. All I did was absorb your training, thank you for it, and then apply it in my businesses in a pragmatic manner. Case closed."

Like I said, this was not an ideological battle being waged between Jason and me; this was just between him and me period. I am proud of Jason's success despite what his mother says but I am disappointed in his life choices.

Four

On Wednesdays I walk the streets of San Francisco, my mind filled with reminiscences and hope, the way a garden is filled with both flower buds and the promise of spring. It is the day I visit Jason, Sally, and the grandkids. I strive to make it a civil visitation, directing all my energies to that end starting when I get up the morning. I put on a pot of very strong coffee and while it is brewing I go over to V-J to grab a banana and a sweet bun, saying my helloes to any neighbors I run into, some of whom I have known all my life. I like having close neighbors. I like having known them continuously for more than seven decades.

"Hi, Marty."

"Hi, Lois."

"How are the kids?"

"Fine. And yours?"

"Fine."

Lois, a heavy-set, grey-haired lady is a widow and an amateur San Francisco historian. She loves to hang out in family owned and run coffee shops reading alternate newspapers and making disparaging comments about their content. That is OK with me. Lois and I went to grammar school together and I was a friend of her dear departed husband Louis. Louis and Lois, they were a pair. They were never too keen on Sophia because of her age disparity with me but I couldn't blame them for that. Anyway, I said hello to Lois this morning but without letting her trap me into a long-winded conversation about the good old days, had my breakfast, read a little Austin, that is John and not Jane, wrote a few sentences on an article I suspect will never get finished, and now here I am out walking.

I could say I know every street in this town intimately and that I never tire of seeing them again but that last conjunct turns the whole sentence into an exaggeration if not a falsehood; still and all this is a good city to walk in if one is inclined to walk at all. Since I walk every day I have long been in the habit of varying my particular route so that I get to where I am going in circuitous ways. Sophia used to walk with me and, while I used the sights and sounds of San Francisco to inspire my inner spirit, my wife was exclusively into real estate.

"Look at that, Marty! That is the third time this year they hung the for sale sign out."

I was not interested in buying and selling houses, or splitting them up into condos, or into individual rooms, much less combining them again into single houses. Sophia on the other hand was hopeless on this topic: her interests were and still are banal.

"Why do you point that out to me, Sophia? Do you want to *buy* it?"

"Oh, Marty, why do you have to be so negative? We *could* buy it. We could paint it up and …"

"What?"

"Resell it."

I looked sideways at her. She was pouting. Sophia looked very sexy when she pouted. I will give the woman that.

Today I walked down Taylor to Post, turned right, then continued on Post to Webster Street where I turned right again. Not a fancy, zigzag route I will admit but what can I say; the really, really twisted patterns I choose at random bore me as much as do these simple ones of late; one can only treat a big city as a state of mind or as a metaphor for the whole world, or as a microcosm of the macrocosm for so long and then one must face the physical facts; San Francisco can be walked a thousand times over if you live as long as I do in this one place.

Jason and his family live on Webster Street just off Broadway in Pacific Heights. They bought two adjacent, freestanding town houses and combined them into a single edifice painted all the colors the Victorians could think up. For my money the house stands out like those storefronts in Amsterdam where the ladies of the red light district parade their wares in windows but I say nothing; I am the quiet, all suffering, misunderstood and unrecognized liberal. Just because Jason and Sally looked in some fifty-dollar coffee table book and found a Victorian mansion that had the porch railings painted in three shades of red and the window sills in green, gold, and blue, and even if every paint color was authentic, it doesn't mean the Victorians knew what they were about.

Anyway, Jason is a good husband and father. If he is in town working and not on a trip he makes sure he is home for an early supper every single day. That usually means he is back working after that early supper but it matters not; his children treasure his time and attention and his wife understands the demands of his schedule.

I did not mean to characterize Jason as some sort of omnipresent store clerk. In truth he does not spend his days in his many stores anymore unless he is personally inspecting. He has an office in a skyscraper at the Embarcadero Center where he monitors shipments of goods coming in from China, deals with headaches generated by international suppliers and their tales of shortages, and devotes himself to the intricacies of doing business in California including negotiating the tax codes, the revenue streams and the mounds of paperwork. He is also branching out into Nevada and, these days, takes private jets to Las Vegas to talk screws and lips. I stay out of the picture. That is Jason's *real* business; the last thing I would do is to interfere with my son's concerns on any serious level. Besides, I have no idea how high-level business works. My quarrel with Jason remains on the conceptual level. *How* he became successful is his worry and God bless him. *That* he became successful by distinguishing between a ten-penny nail and a brad is something else. That is how I see it.

The inside of the Parrish house on Webster Street is impressive. Sally has stuffed it full of Chinese antiques and French furniture. Again my son and his wife slavishly followed instructions out of some book but this time I approve and never fail to say as much; their taste reminds me of my parents taste, and God knows I am comfortable living in my own house.

Jason is thirty-eight years old. Like me he has blue eyes and a pale complexion, though the resemblance stops there. He gets his good looks, his size, and his athleticism from his mother's side of the family. He stands six feet three, a full six inches taller than me, and he has a full head of hair, something I truly envy, for I am bald above the ears. His wife Sally is a big-boned girl, a jolly lady with blonde hair and fleshy arms who is forever letting loose with a hearty laugh and who maintains an uncritical attitude towards life, something she will keep up so long as the supply parts business prospers I would hazard, though I would never say such a thing aloud. Sally and I get along well with one another. She never starts arguments with me like Jason does and she is quick to offer me seconds when we are all seated at the dining table. I do like my food I will admit. That was one bone of contention I had with Sophia; she was always trying to get me to diet.

Jason and Sally have two children, a boy named Michael, who is eight, and a girl named Susan, who is seven. I like them well enough though it pains me to know that Jason has them programmed.

"Grandpa, why are you so crotchety?" Michael will say for no reason at all. Susan is worse: she raises her voice to me assuming I am deaf. Both kids treat me as if I am senile as well, though Jason says that is all in my head.

"Dad! The kids love you."

I guess. Yet I do resent it when people say I exaggerate. I enjoy these early dinners at the big house on Webster Street. I wish I had married a woman like Sally instead of one like Sophia but then again I was the one who had it all figured out back in the sixties. I still believe that a man can mold his wife for the better but would never dare say that in public. I'd be accused of being a male chauvinist or worse.

During dinner I looked out over the table and I fairly ached with love. I do not miss Sophia now that she has left me but that does not mean I am not lonely; in fact I prefer being alone while being lonely too, that is a juggling act comes with being over seventy. My friend, the widow Lois, has hinted that we could do some traveling together once my divorce comes through but I demur; even though I am round and bald and look more like a man of eighty than I do my own age I have my vanity; I can no more see myself walking down some street in Europe with grey-haired Lois on my arm than I can with one of those ancient Chinese women who negotiate the hills of San Francisco with their tiny steps. I'd consider a girl like Sally; she would make me feel young.

"More meat, Marty?"

"Thank you."

I stayed as long as I could and would have stayed longer, but Jason had to get back to work.

"Drop you at home, Dad?"

"No, no, no, I want to walk."

I took Jackson Street heading home and by the time I arrived back at my place I was disgruntled. I lit a cigarette but put it out because it tasted acrid. I mixed myself a Seven and Seven, then poured it down the sink because it tasted flat.

OK. Jason and Sally have not asked me to move in with them. Even if they did I would say no: I would tell them that I am not *that* old. It is just that I am retired, bored and out of sorts.

Jason is my favorite. My other children give me heartburn. I love them all equally of course, it is just that when I come home from visiting Jason I feel so *wistful* that I have no arguments to offer in my own defense. If the human species were not endowed with intelligence we would still love one another and feel wistful at times I am sure; it is just that there would be no need for logic teachers.

Five

I am not a curmudgeon. I forgive these misunderstandings my family has about me. I have been blindsided so many times by my children I have come to expect it, though I am proud to say I am the quiet martyr. My second child, Judy, one of the worst offenders, was born in 1972 and is now thirty-six years of age. She is not married.

Even as a little girl Judy was one who knew exactly what she wanted. She wanted the best, though what she considered the best I judged to be the worst. She wanted the most expensive dolls, the loudest wallpaper put up in her room, the whitest socks, the snappiest gum, the grungiest sneakers, grungy sneakers being the fashion, and the biggest and brightest hair rollers. She would scream her lungs out if she couldn't have *all* her girlfriends staying over at our place weekends.

Nothing changed when Judy grew into a teenager. She went around wearing the latest and gaudiest designer jeans. She sang advertising jingles non-stop, causing me to put plugs in my ears, and worst of all she got nauseous whenever I tried to teach her the rudiments of logic. I am being literal here. Judy would vomit when I insisted she sit down at the kitchen table and turn sentences into symbols. Judy persisted in being a bratty child and, in mockery of my lessons, was bratty in what amounted to a formal sense of the word.

"*I* am not spoiled, Daddy. *You* are impossible."

What I got from my daughter were not arguments but statements. Judy would say something and then go blithely ahead with that, assuming that her statement was a proven fact to which we all agreed.

She did like to shop. Judy shopped harder and longer than her mother if that was possible. She had a nose for the most expensive boutiques and more than once she talked Sophia into buying and wearing clothes that were unsuitable for a married woman and a mother, though I held my tongue. I made up for the expense by dressing down myself. Judy did not appreciate that.

"You walk around like a bum. Is that how you teach?"

Judy had an edge to her and it was revealed in her use of language. Which was ironic because Judy did exceptionally well in school, even rivaling Jason in her overall grade average. Judy did well while *not* valuing the education she was getting and by *not* adopting its goals. I never could get over that. For example, Judy hated history and never hesitated to badmouth it. The more interesting and poignant the history the more she hated it.

"But darling, Julius Caesar was a pivotal force in this world. He …"

"Oh screw all the Caesars."

Here is the thing. She took this history course in high school and refused to open the book and when the test came she got a score of one hundred. She led the class.

"It is just a bunch of facts to memorize, Daddy. Anybody can do it though why he or she would do so is beyond me. I just did it to make you happy and so you would let me go out weekends."

"Yes, good, but, Judy, you can learn so much about life from the Romans."

"Screw the Romans."

Judy grew up being both smart and anti-intellectual. I wanted to blame Sophia for this but then I remembered that Sophia was anti-intellectual and not all that smart. Judy would never be a scholar but she did like her radio. She played pop tunes with the volume turned up full blast whenever I was preparing for my classes or writing my articles, yet I gave into her to save peace in the family. Judy has a temper. It is worse than my own. When we did fight, when we both raised our voices, it would give Sophia sick headaches and since Judy would not back down I always did. I was a little afraid of my daughter, I will admit.

Her anti-intellectualism spilled over into aesthetics as well. Judy liked TV game shows and laughed in my face when I tried to introduce her to art movies or chamber music. She was bright but shallow, hard-shelled on the outside but harder inside. She was recalcitrant but not at all silly like her younger sister in line, Melissa. Judy's toughness made me shudder.

For years I thought she was simply rebelling against me, her father. Finally I realized there was more to it. Judy was rebelling against everything I stood for, and I thought I stood for what was best in the western philosophical tradition updated to include analytic methodology. That was difficult for me to swallow. That was chilling.

Years went by and though I knew she was rebelling I failed to grasp her motivation for it, or to appreciate its depth. Today I can look back and say that Judy was part of a cutting edge cultural changeover, one I label as bankrupt. Yet that was Judy's choice in this shared life.

The boys found my daughter sexy though I must say she was not really a beauty. She was short and thin and wore too much makeup. She took her facial looks after me but always disguised it; by the time she was seventeen she had already done damage to her hair by over-doing it with perms. She shaved her eyebrows, too. This was not good.

I hate to say this but when Judy was growing up I told Sophia that our daughter had no soul. That was my attempt to be honest but Sophia started crying.

"If you'd try being tolerant with the child, Marty, she would be nicer to you."

"Not tolerant? Me? Me! I am the most tolerant man in San Francisco."

"You think you are, Marty, but you are really being a bastard."

"Look I … I don't say this about Judy lightly. There is something sinister about our second child and I say that *knowing* that I have had nothing whatsoever to do with her turning out the way she has."

"You are blaming me because Judy won't take up logic like you want?"

"No, no, no. God, Sophia, I am not blaming you for Judy."

"You mean you are willing to *pardon* me for her. I know you, Marty. You never give an inch. Your compliments are like little critical darts one takes in the back."

That wasn't fair. Judy, as a teenager, reminded me of those female students I had who signed up for my intro philosophy course because they had to take *some* elective. These were the girls who came into class chewing gum and who slammed their books down on the floor and kept them there. Girls who ran in packs and would move their desks around into a circle so that some of them put their backs to me when I was lecturing and who, when I called them on it, looked at me as if I was a killjoy.

Judy was that kind of daughter. She was the kind of daughter who let me know I was boring without ever stopping to consider that *she* was boring, too. Yet there was more to it in Judy's case. It was not a matter of immaturity, she matured right on time. It was not a case of cultural ignorance, I gave her all the opportunities she needed and she consciously rejected each one in turn. It was something deeper and harder than that.

Then again I feel ashamed writing this. Perhaps I have gone too far in characterizing my second child as being difficult. I do not wish to leave the reader with the impression that Judy is some sort of an evil person. She is not anything like that. I love her. I love Judy for herself and I love her along with the rest of my children in equal measure. I mean that. Judy is not a monster. She never did me any real harm. It is just that what she stands for *is* evil in my estimation. I will have to take a deep breath before explaining that.

Six

Judy was not interested in going to college back east. She went to the University of Washington where two of her girlfriends were attending and there she majored in marketing. I was openly bitter over her choices; that is both the school and the major. Judy remained steadfastly blasé regarding my protests while Sophia defended our daughter every step of the way.

"Let her be, Marty! Let her be!"

I let her be. I just paid the bills and let her be. When I tried to remind her mother of that Sophia shot back,

"Marty, shut up. You may know your figures but you don't know the score."

I did know the score and I was busy adding it up since Judy was a girl. For the longest while I kept up a running battle with my second child regarding the phenomenon known as marketing but soon enough it became clear to me that Judy was not listening to, not responding to, and not respecting my arguments. Over time she would give me that hard bright smile, sigh, chuckle, and then pat me on the shoulder saying:

"Oh, Dad. You should see a doctor."

Marx knew about the big movements but even he would have been stunned to see how corporations and their institutional advertising assaults took over this world, pushing past borders and across cultural lines. American civilization got caught up in a shotgun wedding to brand names and instead of pushing the symbol of the flag first, the brands went first and got wrapped in the flag the way Christmas presents get wrapped in colored paper.

"What's *wrong* with that, dad?"

"I will tell you what is wrong, Judy. What you are studying, what you are doing, what *they* are doing, is destroying epistemology."

"What? Epistemology? What the hell is epistemology? Epistemology! Dad! Give me a break. If you did a survey today and took it into every swamp and hollow across this country, asking people it they heard of epistemology what would the results be? A virtual zero! Dad? Then ask those same folks about Hershey candy bars. No contest. Case closed. End of story."

Judy would return from college for a weekend looking hard and shrewd. She would go so far as to test Sophia and me.

"Mom, Dad. Suppose you had two brands of mayonnaise. Hellmann's and brand X. Would you be inclined to try brand X? Be honest now."

That would start off the weekend. Then we would get the rest of the harangue. We would hear about brand loyalty. Judy's eyes would glaze over when she spoke the term 'brand loyalty'. It was as if that was the only loyalty, or the number one loyalty, or … it was quasi-religious in my estimation. I tried my best of counter her.

"Yes, brand loyalty. But what do you have to say about cigarettes? I read your paper. Cigarettes are cheap to make, addictive, and yet smokers are fiercely loyal to a brand. What about that!"

"OK. The ethics thing you mean. Dad, we covered that stuff. The bottom line in business is profit, right? Ethics can only be above the line. So when ethics works, they use it and then they gain further profit by hyping the fact that they are ethical. It is business, Dad. Business."

Judy was not interested in business per se; she was interested in pushing successful businesses. She and I did have some interesting talks about personal identity. I tried once to introduce her to the theory of John Locke but she laughed at me. Judy's take on personal identity was very different.

"Identity is a badge, Dad. It is a logo. Take the Mercedes Benz logo. *That* is one powerful upscale badge of identity. That is a logo to be proud of, to strive for, to obtain. What is wrong with that? Dad? What better identifies a person, that he or she drives a Benz, or that he or she wasted their time sitting in some dusty library reading the words of a dull man long dead?"

While Judy was in college I began noticing something in my intro philosophy classes. Kids who were majoring in marketing showed a uniform dislike and a hostile resistance to what I was teaching them. Amazing, but if someone was majoring in marketing, philosophy was the enemy. It was not a conscious movement at first, but it was ever growing. There was this mutual hostility and I thought that was significant. These growing pockets of resistance formed a pattern and led to some delicious anecdotal confrontations.

Many students majoring in marketing would do spectacularly poorly in my classes through midterm. Instead of coming to me when I asked them to, to get help, they would absent themselves until just before the final. Then they would return to class, fidget, ask phony questions, drop blanket statements of insincere praise, and the like. Here was the problem. If I let them take the final then their grade would dip from D to F, because they would be sure to flunk the last test. So what I did was this: I called them in to my office one at a time and told them I had a deal for them.

"If you take my final you will flunk the course. But, if you were to disappear starting today, disappear so that I never, ever see your face in my classroom again, and then skip the final, too, I will give you a D. How does that sound?"

They were, every one of them, ecstatic.

I told that story to my daughter and she was torn between being upset and laughing sardonically.

"Dad. You are the worst. You know that?"

"You tell me."

"You are one of those mean old professors who can't stand it when young people pass through your classes and don't … ah … respect you enough."

"You wanted so say, don't kiss my ass."

"Well you said it, not me."

When she was a senior she came home to announce that she was zeroing in on what she called "a logo to die for".

What Judy meant was she was getting recruitment calls from big outfits and was officially on the job market. Sophia was happy for her and even I had to admit there were many, many more opportunities out there for marketing majors than there were for philosophy majors.

"At least you won't be starving."

"Thanks a hell of a lot for that."

During Judy's final year of school we communicated a lot by telephone. She called me collect from Washington State and we discussed what Judy called the "philosophy of marketing." I would rise to the bait: I so hate it when someone uses the word philosophy in that way. Still, I cherished those phone calls.

"The whole of life comes down to what we have been battling over, Judy, darling. The real, intellectual, bottom line movements that crown philosophical history as it gets woven into human history are being overthrown in favor of … what? Designer dresses?"

"Oh, Dad. You just don't understand. Girls like to shop. Women like to shop. It is what *satisfies* us. You just block your ears and close you eyes to the truth. You say you are after the truth but it is just the opposite. You are denying it."

I tried to extend the principle of charity to what my daughter was doing. I agreed to read one of her marketing plans she was putting together for her senior thesis. My God!

"Ain't it complex, Dad?"

"Yes, but complexity is not to do with depth. Spinoza's definitions are … simple but deep and …"

"Spinoza is dead, Dad. He has no influence on the market."

"Yes, but—"

"Dad. When you argue like that it reflects badly on you. It underscores what people think of you."

"You mean I am on my way to becoming an old fart."

"Well … you say these things, not me. But it is true! You are becoming a bore."

"Philosophy is not boring! Just the opposite."

"Dad? Face the facts. Only boring people go to school so that they can sit down to study the stuff you teach. The rest of us are there to fulfill our ambitions."

Judy was beyond my grasp, beyond my influence. She was part of the anti-intellectual movement taking over education. In my day, there were hints of it. Kids would say,

"Why do we have to take Latin, anyway? It's a dead language. Give me something that will get me a good job."

Those kids won the battle and lost the war. They would meet up with some old professor wearing a dirty, wrinkled old rain coat who spoke in a strange affected way about the *Odes* of Horace and go home thinking him quaint but out of touch. They would not fail to remark that he didn't seem to be very affluent. And didn't I go along with them in Jason's case? I did. I taught him logic and not Latin. Yet with Judy it had become a far-reaching implication.

I will say this. I met lots of Judy's college friends. They loved coming into San Francisco for visits, staying for free at our house. They were all decent human beings. They were polite young men and women from loving families who spoke well and who had impeccable manners. They did not go around *being* the hostile people I characterized them as being, for they saw nothing wrong with what they were doing with their lives.

Looking back on it today I can see what was happening. The old 19th Century fear of nihilism was winding down and, in its place was not art, or science, or even technology; it was marketing. And Judy was in the vanguard. She ended up writing her senior thesis on what she called "knockoffs". I read it and was impressed.

"You see, Dad, even poor folks need brands."

I was proud of my daughter while at the same time I found what she was doing chilling. I would be joking with her one minute and filled with horror the next. What upset me the most was that marketing majors never felt the horror. They were too busy memorizing the steps to successful marketing while getting ready to push products and create new markets. I said to my daughter once,

"I mean you are just … a saleswoman, right?"

She looked at me with disgust. In that one second *I* had become the Philistine and she the wounded party.

Later that day Sophia took me aside to tell me that I had hurt our daughter's feelings with my prejudicial comments. I had to apologize. My apology was delivered coldly. I am sorry to this day that I was not more gracious. I guess I should have said something about how philosophers are blind to economic profits, or how everyone needs to spend money, or whatever. I did not.

Judy finished college and *then* moved east, taking up residence in Manhattan and going to work for one of the largest marketing firms in the world. From there she proceeded to build a spectacular career, working as many as eighteen hours a day. Right now Judy is vice-president of operations for a subsidiary firm bent on increasing sales of Coca Cola and McDonald's products in Italy. She divides her time between Manhattan and Milan, is flown around in a private jet, and makes sure she calls both Sophia and me every Christmas to tell us she loves us. She does love us, though from the sound of her voice it is clear that she considers us fuddy-duddies.

Seven

Judy flew to San Francisco last month to visit me and her brothers and sisters. Sophia was invited to fly in from Miami Beach and at first my no good, soon to be ex-wife pretended she couldn't make it because she was going to be tied up with real estate transactions, which was her way of saying that since I did not volunteer to pay for her ticket and Judy didn't think of doing so, she wouldn't come west, not because she was offended, but because she couldn't afford it. I finally paid for Sophia to come and the seven of us had a grand reunion of sorts. Sophia stayed with Jason and Judy stayed with her younger brother, Martin Jr.

We couldn't believe how sophisticated Judy had become. She is still hard looking, but there is no doubt about it, she has that aura of a highly successful woman about her. She drinks too much coffee, eats too little food, hardly sleeps, and keeps going on sheer adrenalin, but in a way it makes her look intriguing. I will admit I was in awe of her.

The kids loved having Judy home. Jason booked the finest restaurants for the family to eat in, Melissa managed to get something said about her on the local news, Cassandra prayed for her, God help us all for that, and Martin Jr. took her off to a political rally. Sophia and I made sure we were never isolated together one on one and we managed not to fight in our children's presence. We pulled it off and, as they say in the passive voice; a good time was had by all.

For her part Judy kept up a bright conversational patter during her entire visit. On the night before she was to go back to Europe, and at her suggestion, she and I went out alone to the St. Regis for an early supper. We were to meet up with the rest of the family for drinks at a wharf restaurant on the Embarcadero around nine p.m. and that gave us plenty of time for a father-daughter get together. I was delighted to do so. It gave us the chance, at last, to sit down together as two adults and, hopefully, not bicker like we used to do when Judy was young. How did I know she wanted to use this time to complain about her love life? We were just getting into our tuna tartar when Judy started in with a rush.

"Men! Dad? Why are you men all the same?"

I put my fork down carefully. I didn't know *what* was coming next but I knew *that* it was coming.

"Now, now, now. Judy? Darling? What is it? What is the matter? Is it something you would be better off discussing with your mom?"

"No! Dad, I am thirty-six years old and unmarried."

"Well, you … wanted a career, didn't you?"

"What does *that* have to do with it? Yes, I want a career. Can't I have a husband and children, too?"

"Of course you can. Why don't you? What is stopping you?"

"Men."

"Now what?"

"Face facts. I make seven hundred grand a year and that doesn't even include my bonuses and my stock options. Does that mean I want to pick up the check when I am out with a guy? No. I want to feel like a woman out on a date."

"Well, I agree. But I am sure that there are loads of men on your level who are dying to date you."

"There are not! Successful men hate successful women. They hate us! They only want to date secretaries. They only want to marry bimbos!"

"Well, what of less successful men?"

"I don't want to go out with guys whom I intimidate. Guys who try to take you to slop houses just because they are watching their pennies. Jesus, Dad, why are you guys so afraid of successful gals?"

I cleared my throat. I was ready for this one. I do listen to public radio. I knew a few things.

"Judy. You are right, anecdotally. You have experienced an old female complaint. But seriously now, statistics show a new trend. Affluent and successful men are more likely to marry affluent and successful women than they are their secretaries. It is just the case."

Well, that turned out to be a false step on my part. My daughter started to yell at me and then she broke down crying. I had hit a sore spot all right. I had sworn not to do anything like that the moment I heard Judy was flying into town yet I had just gone ahead and done so; I was immediately plunged into remorse. With Sophia I *had* behaved myself. With Judy I was once again playing the cad and without meaning to do so.

"Come on, come on," I said impatiently. I didn't mean … Jesus, Judy, I love you."

Judy had a good cry. It lasted five full minutes. I waved the waiter off twice and then sat there scarcely breathing while my daughter made up her mind as to whether she wanted to spend the rest of our dinner together railing against me both as her father and as the representative of the male sex, or whether she wanted to reach out and extract some empathy from me. To my great relief she chose the latter, though I could have done without the details. She started to tell me about her love life.

"I went with this one guy for a year. He is a junior sales rep. He was attentive but oh, *so* passive. He would defer to me on everything. I finally dumped him. I mean you can't … men like that … Dad? He was not argumentative like you are but … gosh … how many times can you come home at night to see a guy sitting there in his underwear drinking beer and watching soccer?"

"Did he drink the right brand of beer?"

"Oh, Dad, you are a scream. You are a real comedian."

For the moment Judy reminded me of herself as a teenager. I was actually feeling nostalgic.

"This guy you dumped, was he your age?"

"No, no. He was only twenty-five."

"Twenty-five! What were you, robbing the cradle?"

"You should talk. Look at Mom."

"Yes but men … ah, oh boy. Here I go. It is just that it is more *natural* for the man to be older."

I couldn't stop myself. I said that and it was the last straw. Judy became angry again but this time she did not follow that up with tears. Instead she reverted to meanness and deliberately tried to embarrass me.

"You know why I like younger men, Dad? Because they are better in bed."

"All right. All right. I got the point. There is no need to be crude."

Judy pulled back but the dinner was ruined and, in a sense, the whole visit was now tainted. Judy and I are just not destined to get along. I couldn't fight it anymore. People can love one another or hate one another and it makes no difference; we are all human beings with our own limitations; we run out of excuses, chances, changes, and surprises; suffice to say that Judy and I will do one another no great harm though we will continue to apply the torture of a thousand cuts.

The final family get-together down at the wharf was sweet and sad. I sat there while my five children chatted mostly with one another, offhandedly assuming that Sophia and I were to be taken for granted.

Then again maybe I was just being too defensive.

Eight

Melissa, my next daughter in line, is now thirty-four. Notice that our children came along every two years; Sophia and I did not plan that, at least as far as I know; Sophia does have a mind of her own though God knows what constitutes it; it certainly does not get folded into Kant's master schema for rational entities.

Anyway, *Melissa's* childhood was one of exaggerated girlishness. Wait. That doesn't quite capture what I mean to say. I am not referring to ideological issues of power the way some people characterize female gender development today. I have quite the opposite idea in mind. What I am trying to convey is the fact that, on the surface, young Melissa never failed to display the cutest poses and adopt the most sugary feminine stances, doing everything she could to show the world she was playing a role that, on the one hand would guarantee her never being taken seriously in a competitive world but, on the other hand would suit her needs perfectly and, furthermore, assure her getting ahead of most of the hardheaded people who saw reality in competitive terms only, so that in the final analysis the joke was on the world and not her.

For all of that girlishness Melissa was never quite daddy's little girl in the traditional sense. I treated her as fairly and as evenly as I did all my children; yet I knew early on and to my ongoing disappointment that Melissa was not, forgive me for this word, *constitutionally* interested in learning about logic, much less about systematic approaches to thinking. I knew symbolic logic; Melissa knew about the color hot pink, though her approach to it was different in kind from Judy's take on the color or her mother's take on the color; Judy could sell it, Sophia would buy it, but Melissa identified with it.

Melissa, like other females in our family, was not really beautiful, though she was persistently cute. Her face was one people never tired of looking at, yet no one would have suggested she go off to model down a ramp or try out for Hollywood movies. She had an ever-pleasing face, a ready smile, and was quick to giggle. From the start she perfected a waitress or airline stewardess approach to life; she let others, be they male or female, rule the conversation and set the tone while she ran around supplying pillows and extra cups of coffee; she bolstered other people's egos while never letting you take your eyes off her.

Ah, yes. Listen to your self, Marty! You are the one who fought off each and every ideological invasion by remaining the silent and tolerant liberal, and now here you are delivering what amounts to a negative critique of your own flesh and blood *just because* she never got drawn into one of these movements herself. Melissa did not get taken seriously but that has proven to be her strength, if one does couch success in certain terms.

Certain terms? Face it. I am disappointed in the way my daughter Melissa turned out because she grew up as an uncritical fan of the popular culture and has never left off doing so. Yes, I can and I do rail against both radical movements and the status quo at the same time. What I wanted for my kids and did not get was something altogether different.

I wanted them to be, well, more like me.

I don't mean more like me on the surface, much less personality-wise. I wanted them to be able to see the fault lines running through society the way one can spot earthquake fault lines running close by the Golden Gate Bridge. I wanted them to be logical, damn it. They didn't have to become professional logicians necessarily though I would have thrilled to that; yet it would have been nice if at least one of my children had gained some distance from our society and our culture instead of merely participating in it.

I guess I am accusing my child of never having gained anything like true self-consciousness.

I couldn't blame Sophia for how Melissa turned out and I never tried doing so. I looked to myself instead, not that it did me any good. I just floundered about doing what I always did; I stood askance of my daughter, wondering how she could have proceeded from our loins. I am talking about a deep human mystery here. I am talking about a mystery that without any effort makes a mockery out of the intellectual parameters philosophers have always tried to place the world within.

How many times did I come home from the university, my head filled with the finest philosophical distinctions, to find Melissa standing in front of the mirror in the hallway holding up two dresses, one with big black and white polka dots, the other with big yellow sunflowers and, upon seeing me, turn to me and say,

"What do you think, Daddy? The black and white or the yellow and white?"

At such times I would be plunged into an all too familiar crisis. I just could not make the comfortable transition from giving myself over to my profession all day long, to being at home with my scatterbrained daughter. There had to be, in my judgment, something to unify both enclaves and yet there was not any such glue to be had; it was enough to turn me into an existentialist, though I am happy to report that I conquered that temptation.

Socrates said, famously, that the unexamined life is not worth living. More than one female student of mine challenged that one over the years but I always managed to dismiss such outcries as mere immature mumblings. With Melissa, Socrates might have met his match.

I am being serious. Nietzsche is infamous for his attacks on Socrates. Melissa, without knowing it, might have done the old Greek much more damage. She was a super-feminine girl and that sufficed for her in ways that still leave me breathless. So who am I to say that her life is not worth living? I love my daughter after all.

Melissa went to San Francisco State but never came remotely near a class I taught. As to what she majored in, I suppose one can call it by what it has become known as today under the official title, communications, though that word makes me rage inside. Melissa and I never argued over anything when she was a girl, yet when she got to college I found myself sniping at her and much to her surprise.

Here is the most galling thing: while Melissa took a gentle and bantering approach in answering me she, and at the same time, literally began talking down to me; she actually went out of her way to show patience with what she took to be her doddering parent. She would explain to me that I was “out of touch”, a “dinosaur”, “an old white guy”, “not hip”, “not with it”, and the like: she even took it upon herself to tell to me how the new generation “worked” and why the old generation did not. One time our conversation took a critical turn while I was hanging around her room as she applied makeup to her face.

“It is like this, Dad. You grew up using your whole body to communicate, like an actor in a theater. Nowadays there are talking heads. I am the perfect talking head in the making. I am cute. You could never survive in the world the way it is today. Dad? Admit it. You are ready for the dog track.”

“Thank you for that.”

Melissa laughed. Then she added more mascara to her already plastered eye lashes the way a philosopher would run to his source books to gather in more arguments.

Nine

Today, Melissa is co-anchor of the so-called ten a.m. edition of the morning news on a local television station here in San Francisco. Ratings are high. Her partner, Millie, is a woman made out of cardboard. I would say the same about Melissa but do not because I incidentally know better; I have insider information that Melissa happens to be made out of flesh and blood because she is my own flesh and blood.

Melissa and Millie deliver softballs for a living, that is to say they take turns reading monitors wherein pseudo news is handed out over the digital highway to stay at home women who would change the channel should anything serious ever dare be discussed. Sponsors see to it that this does not happen, for in this business life imitates commercials.

Melissa covers stories about devotional pets that one can dress up in red woolen sweaters if the weather turns cold, recipes that promise to make food both nutritious and tasty *and* help you lose weight, celebrity gossip in which a single story about a single infidelity attributed to the latest pop singer can be dragged out for three months, and stories about women feeling good about themselves, women communicating with women, and women networking with women. These last stories stretch both the concept of what news is as well as the meaning of faux concepts; Melissa once best described what she does as:

"Exploring what women think about women who are thinking about women."

In my day, if I can say that without agreeing with Melissa that I am a dinosaur, there was a section of every daily newspaper called the "woman's page". It was chock full of household advise, recipes for summer, shopping hints, celebrity gossip and the like; in other words it catered to exactly the same audience that Melissa caters to today. So the woman's page has gone high tech, though there is one difference I ought mention. In my day a woman reporter made next to nothing; today Melissa pulls down two hundred thousand a year.

Around town people talk about Melissa and Millie and what great buddies they are, though the two young ladies do not socialize off camera. Millie is involved in a contract dispute with the station and is jealous of Melissa because Melissa makes more money. Their competition is played out in hairstyles and makeup, though Melissa has retained a lawyer just in case. She refers to Millie in private as:

"A clawing cat."

Now and again I cannot help myself and make some reference to the feminist movement for good or ill, but Melissa cares nothing for that and is quick to say so.

"Daddy? I just went to college, learned how to speak in front of a camera, and got a job. Why do you make such a conspiratorial story out of that? I am *not* an angry woman and I am *not* anti-male. Most of all I am not a feminist."

"Yes, but, you must hear criticism about your news show from women who …"

"Dad? Your concerns only reflect on *you.* I didn't do anything to you as a woman. You have trouble with women. Why don't you admit it?"

I stared at Melissa in disbelief when she said this to me. I was angry and hurt. It is bad enough that I have been unfairly portrayed as a curmudgeon in my own household for years; it was something else that my third child would gratuitously throw in that I was a chauvinist and a misogynist, too.

Melissa's additions stuck. My wife and my other children began using my gender and my age as "proof" of my misogynist nature. Suddenly *I* was the problem, not our evolving western culture. I was soon enough caught up in a vicious circle. I should have know better since I taught courses on how ideology works but what could I do?

About this time I had a male student stand up in one of my classes to tell me that women are victims and men are exploiters, so, whenever a woman did something wrong she could not have done something wrong. Why, because women were victims. When I pointed out the obvious circularity of that argument the whole class piped up, declaring me a chauvinist, adding that even if one could *prove* that a woman did something wrong that still wouldn't add up to her having to be punished, because this is a man's world and woman are forced to comply with it against their wishes. When I tried to tell that story at home Sophia took me by the arm, lead me into the bedroom and whispered,

"Let it go, Marty. You are just making an old fool of yourself in front of the kids."

But to get back to Melissa's morning TV show; it is too, too sugary to watch. She gets to the studio at six a.m. and the crew spends hours doing her hair and makeup, dressing her, and trying different lighting on her. Then she goes on camera and buries the city in trivia.

I will say, at the risk of committing an oxymoron, that my daughter is good at what she does. She is, right this moment, being considered for a slot on a nationally syndicated network show. If she gets that she will without doubt end up a multi-millionaire. This money factor troubles me. No, I am not jealous of Melissa's financial success. On the contrary, I applaud her. What does upset me, philosophically speaking, is that her values succeed while Socrates' values are today all but buried for good. Still, if this is a war between Melissa's values and the values of Socrates, who am I to interfere? My family will say it was because I am a disgruntled old man. I would counter that with something devastatingly logical but I must face facts; they have heard all my counter arguments and none of them have stuck, impressed, or won the day.

Ten

Melissa lives in Cow Hollow, not far from Jason and Sally if you discount the steep plunge one has to take if one is walking from Pacific Heights towards the Union Street Shops. I have dinner with her once a week as well but I don't know how long this will continue. The bald truth of the matter is I cannot stand Melissa's husband.

Mitch. That is his name. Who in hell would ever go around calling himself "Mitch"? I said that to Melissa when she first starting going with him and she turned on me at once.

"Well, who in hell would go around calling himself Marty?"

"Marty is an OK name for a guy. Mitch is … I don't know … it sounds affected."

"Daddy! That is just stupid. And you know it."

Well, I figured, better to carp about his name than about the man himself.

Mitch is the local TV weatherman at the station where Melissa works. I ask you: what kind of a job is that for a man? I swear Mitch never takes off his makeup: he walks around that apartment looking like a fancy boy with his trendy clothes while talking up his low carb diets and his workout routines. Melissa won't hear about it. She always shuts me up when I make cracks.

"I pick our Mitch's clothes, Daddy. I won't have him going around town dressed like a bum like you do."

"I dress down because students today expect it."

"Rubbish!"

I don't like any of the new styles in clothing and I don't like the furniture Melissa and Mitch have in their apartment. It looks like kitsch to me. Well, not kitsch like you would find in Switzerland, but, I don't know, I do not like chairs that have that "industrial look", or exposed pipes; I cannot see having all that stainless steel about, and the lighting is all those miniatures that shine spots in my eyes no matter where I sit or stand in the place.

Every time I come for dinner I do so having vowed to hold my tongue. I make that vow as I walk from Nob Hill towards Russian Hill before swinging left to get to their place. Not only do I promise to hold my tongue, I promise to be polite as well. I break my vows every time I get there, usually while working on my second cocktail. Last month for example I really let it out. I didn't attack Melissa and Mitch personally; I went after the moguls who employ them.

"Doesn't it make you two feel even a little bit guilty to know that no more than a half a dozen right-wing businessmen control the media world wide? Doesn't it bother you that they are keeping the masses of humanity in ignorance while they rake in obscene amounts of profit? They don't give us news; they give us pabulum."

Melissa countered this by batting her eyelashes in mock innocence and saying,

"As far as I am concerned, Daddy, men make the decisions in this world and that does not trouble me at all. I am the girl. I do what comes naturally."

Which was Melissa's way of telling me that if I wanted to argue, I should do it with her husband. I cannot stand arguing with Mitch. I think he is a lightweight. I know I am risking my daughter's anger here but I do not give a damn. I depreciate everything coming out of Mitch's mouth. Worse, he argued reasonably during the visit.

"Marty? Listen to yourself. Your ideas about the media do not progress. They are nothing but goddamn sound bites. You never advance them. You heard once about the collapsing together of media outlets and you decided you were against it and yet you never bothered to look into it. Tell me if I am wrong."

"You are right but it makes no difference. The news is no more. The news has asked Americans to turn inward. Why, you guys have no one in the field. You have no reporters, just talking heads delivering opinions."

Mitch countered by defending the talking head turn. He actually got angry with *me.* He actually thinks Americans *ought* to turn inward because the world is a dreadful, dreary, and unworkable place. I heard this and I wanted to toss my drink in his face. What a lightweight!

By the time we sat down to dinner I had managed to apologize to Mitch for losing my temper and he did the same. We shook hands. His hand feels like a manikin's hand but that is neither here nor there. Someone suggested once that I harbor trapped father-daughter feelings for Melissa and that despite what I say about even-handedness, she really was daddy's girl but I doubt it; I treated all my kids the same. It is just that I feel so stupid for having to goad my daughter into being more of a feminist. Even during this visit nothing changed; I held my tongue until served my salad, then mumbled:

"That woman who … ah … Christiane Amanpour … something or other… she is a reporter I really respect. She is out *covering* the war and bringing real news into our living rooms and …"

Melissa snapped back:

"Daddy, I do not do that sort of stuff. That is not what I do."

"I know but listen; I was not talking about you. I was talking about the lack of real news coverage in the media. Why when I was a kid we had all that reporting on the war coming to us from every country in Europe. We had short wave and you could turn that dial and get reporters giving news from London and from the front and …"

"Daddy! The war? You mean like the German war? Oh, daddy, stop showing your age. People don't do that anymore. It is bad form."

"Bad form? I … Melissa … what will you be doing for the network if you get this job?"

"I might be allowed to cover the Olympics from the studio back in America."

"Cover it? Cover sporting events?"

"No, no, Dad. It is not really about sporting events. It is about bringing a female audience aboard for two weeks. Women don't like sports and don't follow them. Men do that. So once every four years women rule: that is the real Olympic spirit. These viewers don't want sports; they want sentimental stories about the competitors. That is what sells products."

"I suspected as much."

"Daddy! You are wrong it you think it is horrible. It is peachy. Like, did you see that McDonald's commercial where someone holds the door open for the old man and he is so grateful? We did a survey and found that millions of women break down crying when they see that commercial. That is what does it today. You don't understand. That is good! If you don't believe me, call up Judy and ask her."

"What is good? That products sell? If that is what good means these days then I truly am a dinosaur, though I would rather be on my way to extinction than on board with sentimentality."

Melissa began to pout and Mitch, ever so sickly cool, jumped in.

"Marty, you mentioned short wave radios. Think about it. *You* made the transition from short wave radio to black and white television, then to color TV, then to VCR's, and on to DVD's. Suddenly *you* have come to a halt while technology keeps marching on. What does that say about you, Marty? Marty, if someone asks you if you are sound system guy or an iPod guy, what would you say?"

"I'd tell them to read Quine."

"Who the hell is he?"

"A guy who knew his logic."

"Oh, Marty. Melissa has told me stories about you. How you used to leave books all around the house hoping your kids would … read them."

I looked at Mitch. He is a little too thin. I said, through clenched teeth,

"It is not *intelligence* that has declined in this world, it is quality of life that has declined."

"What do you mean? Are you saying that high definition television is of lower quality than your old short wave?"

"You miss my point."

Mitch was getting ready to demean me again when Melissa, a bright smile on her face, announced:

"Dad? Guess what. I am pregnant."

I was flabbergasted. Melissa went on to say that the station where she worked planned to launch a new segment that would record her visits to her doctor, would record her and Mitch's taking parenting courses, and so forth. She added,

"Even the network where I might work is excited. They said that if they hire me, it would be good to see a pregnant woman giving lead-ins to real human-interest stories."

Finally I managed to get out,

"You are going to have a baby! That's … great!"

Mitch then harangued my ears with talk about how they were going to take advantage of new technology to monitor the pregnancy and so forth but I tuned him out. I went home that evening feeling older than my seventy-two years. I couldn't help thinking that when this new grandchild was born, and when he or she grew up, the likelihood that they would be reading articles I wrote was not something to bet on.

Eleven

Our fourth child, Cassandra, was, of all our five offspring, most estranged from both Sophia and me, yet there was never anything like a raging conflict or an obvious rebellion we could point to so as to help us put a label on this growing distance; Cassandra simply grew up starting in the late seventies and, I suspect, drew her formative values from the ideological waves then sweeping through the country with its most concentrated essences located here in San Francisco, incorporating them into her self in a way I personally found hard to fathom knowing what I do about the logic of identity. I cannot tell you how many times I wanted to pick Cassandra up in my arms, shake her oh so gently, and whisper,

"Darling, don't take all that stuff seriously. They are just playing with your mind. They are just amassing tiny bits of power for themselves. Best to roll your eyes and move on."

Cassandra did agree to my giving her lessons at home. She wouldn't sit for logic instruction, mind you, but she did ask me to teach her some metaphysics. Though here is the thing: she took in what I had to say while, simultaneously, *deflecting* my help the while. Let me explain that in more detail

While my daughter *was* interested in what I had to say about metaphysics, her interest was not at all concept based, but was, instead, faith orientated. She would break from the lessons to say things like,

"Daddy, faith is fundamental to the human being. Why do you have to keep putting it in these … what are you calling them … abstract terms? You make them sound so harsh. You remind me of a guy I saw on television once. He wore a loud suit and had a cigar in his mouth and he was selling ladies underwear. Yes, he was a salesman all right but he had no feeling for the feeling of underwear against the skin."

I tried to explain.

"The whole of religion is formulated from concepts, darling. What people do is make this mistake: they grant existential existence to that which is not related to any concrete object."

"You are wrong, Daddy. Faith makes us human."

"Well, OK, if you say so, but … ah … we don't *know* what is out there and …"

"Daddy. I will pray for you. You are troubled."

There you have it. Cassandra was going to be one of *those* people. She was focused on some fuzzy feeling or other; she was my daughter and yet she was anti-intellectual. She was not anti-intellectual in the sense my wife was, or in the sense Melissa was, or in the sense Judy was; Cassandra insisted on turning the truth inside out, which was much more serious a mistake in my estimation. She was religious within a tradition of *piety,* something that always rubbed me the wrong way.

"Cassandra? One cannot just believe. One must question."

"I will pray for you, Daddy. You poor soul."

For a long time Sophia and I worried about Cassandra. We feared she might go off and be a nun somewhere, one of those sisters of the suffering masses, one of those selfless creatures who would always manage to make us feel guilty whenever we forked a big piece of steak into our mouths. Yet by the time she got to high school Cassandra's agenda began unfolding in a way that I could finally read. She started registering complaints.

"You write articles, Daddy. Why have you never taken up the real cause of the priesthood?"

"What are you talking about, dear?"

"The Catholic Church, Daddy. They do not allow women to be priests."

"What, ah … that is not a question that interests me. I mean … really."

"It interests me."

"Yes, well, there is a long story to tell about the Catholic Church and the, ah, well, look, you can stand aside and have a chuckle at their expense. I mean …"

"Daddy, there you go again. Putting down the faithful."

Sophia and I would confer and invariably end up shaking our heads. Where was Cassandra getting all these notions? Where was she coming from? We were, by the way, not a religious family. I did not come from a background where anyone went to church, nor did my wife. We didn't poke fun of religion, nor did we go out of our way to express a live and let live policy towards those who trooped off every Sunday morning to some big building. It simply did not take up any space in our minds.

I said I was a silent liberal. I suppose that sort of tolerance was applied unconsciously to religious folk as well. I just never thought of it until Cassandra came along. So maybe it was true that she *did* get all this religious stuff and all this priest stuff from the passing waves of ideology. Knowing what Melissa does for a living makes it somewhat plausible, though, as I indicated above, it befuddles me to have to grant identity status to one who swallows that sort of surface noise.

Cassandra kept up her priest patter while Sophia and I began directing our concerns elsewhere. Cassandra, as she moved through high school, made choices that worried us and though I left it to Sophia to counsel the child, it was obvious that these mother-daughter talks were going nowhere.

Our child started wearing odd clothing. I do not know how else to say it. It was the case. She preferred going around in those full body workman's jeans, the kind that have straps going over one's shoulders like an old time carpenter might wear. Under this she wore woolen shirts you might see on a guy going hunting. She stopped combing her hair, too. She didn't cut it short; she just let it grow indifferently. I swear, when Cassandra and Melissa were standing side by side, or when Judy came into a room where Cassandra was standing, or even when Cassandra was out and about with her mother, I couldn't believe my eyes. This is difficult for me to talk about. This is a real test of my liberalism. Sophia was the one who broke with Cassandra back then. I was the one who defended my daughter against my wife's shrieking outbursts. Yet you know how these things go: when all was said and done, when it came time to parcel out the blame, it all fell solely on my shoulders.

"She is *your* daughter, Marty. *You* are the one gave her those lessons."

"Sophia, please. There is no use turning this on me. Cassandra is who she is. We have to get over it."

Sophia and I had been drifting apart for a long, long while. If she wanted to use our daughter Cassandra's development as an excuse to leave me down the line, then I said to myself,

"So be it."

I love my children equally and evenly. I couldn't help it if our household was going off in seven different directions at once. This point would be better emphasized if I had sat down to write a drama instead of this narrative; I would have been better able to let the reader see what a circus was playing under our roof. As it is, I am dealing with what happened to my children and my wife one at a time. It is best as far as details are concerned.

Twelve

Cassandra went to San Francisco State and then on to the Union Theological Seminary back east. I thought I got it.

"OK, darling. You want to be a minister. You have my blessing."

I said this in a jocular tone to let my daughter know that I was the tolerant father. And why wouldn't I be? I have lots of friends and colleagues who picked up ministerial degrees; some of them even do part time work in some congregation or other. They work their day jobs and then they do their minister stuff on weekends the way some people go sailing on Sundays. I judge it to be a workable solution for them. They got sidetracked as children by this religious hocus-pocus and couldn't completely pull out of it without causing themselves psychological damage, so they handled it in a socially responsible manner and made it their hobby.

I was wrong.

"Dad, I am not going to be a minister. I mean to be a priest."

"Oh, Jesus, Cassandra. Let's get serious."

"Don't take the name of the Lord in vain, daddy."

"Ah … sorry. What I am saying to you is: the Catholic Church is not going to back down in your lifetime and let in female priests."

"I know that."

"Well?"

"I see my opportunity in the Episcopal Church."

She had me there. There was such a movement going on. I was just not prepared to learn that Cassandra meant to jump on that bandwagon. I managed to hold my fire. I embraced my daughter, told her I loved her, and wished her luck. Sophia on the other hand was mortified.

Curiously enough, Cassandra seemed totally immune to what her mother felt or thought. She consistently blanketed both her parents with what I called "faith-based love", it sort of reminded me of the way missionaries overlooked the nakedness of their aboriginal flocks in the beginning. Cassandra began speaking down to both of us and in turn was too far above us to get offended by anything we might say to her.

She did what she had to do. She jumped through all the hoops. She broke barriers. She lobbied. She networked. She cajoled. She moved from diocese to diocese. She sought out mentors. She played politics. In time Cassandra became a female priest. Currently she is assigned to an Episcopal church in the Castro neighborhood here in San Francisco. It was only at this point that my tolerance began being tested in earnest. In other words, it is only recently that I got through to Cassandra so that my arguments have sting. I had better lay this latest development out carefully.

Once Cassandra came back to live in the city and to take on a prominent and very visible role in the Episcopal Church, one that garnered headlines all over the country and the world, Sophia absented herself from the fray. Up to this point she had sniped at our daughter whenever she had her on the telephone or whenever she came to visit. Now that Cassandra had a position to uphold, her mother instinctively turned the battle over to me. I was not happy with this.

"What do you want *me* to say to her, Sophia? I already gave her my blessing. Why don't you do the same and we can both let it go?"

"You are the father. You are the one with the degrees. You deal with it."

"I am *not* going to be dealing with it."

"Famous last words, Mr. Combatant."

It just was not fair. The rest of my children joined in with their mother and began to do two things: blame me for "what happened" to Cassandra, and blame me for "not embracing Cassandra's lifestyle".

It was a typical lose-lose position I was being slotted into; once you are your family's designated curmudgeon then you are damned no matter what.

I am no psychoanalyst. If I unconsciously contributed to Cassandra's becoming what she has become, and if my kids and wife want to blame me for that, then I will just let them. What can I do about that? But the very idea that I don't love my daughter as much as I do the other kids and that this is so because I disapprove of her life and lifestyle in some way when in fact I am a liberal is, well, and as I said, it just is not fair.

I suppose the idea is this: someone has to be the designated fall guy in every society and in every family. I am that someone. I even said as much to Cassandra. She got a good laugh out of it.

"We never really argued, Daddy. I knew what I wanted from the start. You were a sweet guy, really. In your own clumsy way."

I found that reassuring. Yet everyone else in the family kept the pressure on without admitting they were doing so. They would not admit it, but they expected me to *reach* Cassandra in some way that would convey their deepest prejudices while letting me take the heat. Cassandra, daughter of Priam, was a prophetess whose divinations were not to be believed. The rest of my family was maneuvering me into letting *our* Cassandra know just why she was just as cursed. That did not make me into any sort of an Apollo; though it did seal my fate as being the disagreeable old man of Nob Hill.

It is with a full sense of shame that I tell you what I told my daughter one day when, apropos of nothing, I reached way, way down to tell her what I *really* thought about her being a priest.

"Every heard of the Waltari thesis, Cassandra dear?"

"No, but … ah … are you talking about Mika Waltari, the Finnish novelist?"

"Yes."

"I know a few things about him. He was a Christian novelist. He had a daughter. His novel, *The Egyptian,* was the largest selling foreign novel in this country for decades. But as for the 'Waltari thesis', I don't …"

"I made that term up. I took the idea from a throwaway line in the novel you mention."

"What about it, Dad?"

"This. Whenever women take over an institution it is a sure sign that the institution is dead."

Cassandra looked at me. I never saw that look on her face before. I knew I should have stopped right there but for some reason I did not, Cassandra and I had never seriously argued, and nothing I had ever said to her had hurt her. This would be different. I would do this to her *for* the sake of the rest of the family and then, once I did so, my family would distance themselves from me. Finally my daughter did respond.

"I guess I do not follow you, Dad. You mean like, now that we have women lawyers and doctors, that the legal profession and the practice of medicine are finished?"

"Nothing like that. They are professions, not institutions."

"Give me an example of an institution."

"Religion."

"Was that Waltari's own example?"

"Yes."

"What are you trying to tell me?"

"That when St. Augustine was a bishop Christianity was the dominant force growing in the world. Today that force has waned except for political reasons. That is why they let women force their way into the priesthood. They haven't the power to stop them. Now there is nothing left but these sectarian squabbles about … well … issues that have nothing to do with whether or not there is a God up in the sky."

"You really think that, Dad?"

"I do. I think that the concepts of God and the soul have naught to do with social issues in this world. Religion, true religion, doesn't even have to do with the ethics of this world. The very idea that priests are only there to do good deeds of charity or to minister either to the poor or to the ideological interests of certain imploding power groups is … ah … anti-religious in my opinion."

Cassandra said nothing for the longest while. I began to feel terrible. What had I said to my daughter and why had I said it? When she spoke again I suddenly knew two things. First, the emotional separation between father and daughter had finally and irrevocably taken place. Second, Cassandra had survived it. She was who she was and I was the curmudgeon.

"Dad? You lack faith. I feel sorry for you and I will pray for you."

We left it at that. As expected, the rest of my kids and my wife detected a certain coolness now existing between Cassandra and me and they were merciless in letting me know about it. Jason said to me,

"What did you say to my sister? Did you put her down, Dad?"

"Put her down? Listen. I am the only one who accepts Cassandra for who she is."

No one believed me.

Thirteen

My weekly dinners with Cassandra and her "spouse" can perhaps best be categorized as *gentle* events; on the surface we three are totally relaxed sitting around the table with one another while, down deep, we are like a trio of exhausted riders trying to stay with the peloton of a bike race during a category one climb. We follow rules of politeness. We tacitly agree to the point of insistence that polite conversation is different from politically correct conversation. We three strive to close in on what is universally noble in our fellow human beings in the generic sense of the term, thus our conversations are designed to lock in on that humanity so that we can share it with one another while we pass the basket of rolls, simultaneously issuing asides about the firmness of the green beans. This juggling act is not easily done. We three must pre-form the sentences issuing from our lips so that, and while we are ever indicating or suggesting linguistic depth the words themselves remain shameless markers of the banal.

"More cauliflower, Marty?"

"Oh, thank you, Christi. I can't resist that bit of brown sugar you rub on the flowers."

"I don't rub, Marty. I buy them all set to go."

"Whatever."

Up until a few months ago our family referred to Christi as Cassandra's lesbian lover. No more. Those two got married last week under current California law, though I wouldn't go to the bank on that legislation standing up to anything like a real challenge. Melissa disagrees.

"Face it, Dad, you are not keeping up on what is going on in the world. The world has moved on. You have not."

Maybe she is right in this one case. Cassandra, my priest-daughter, and her spouse, Christi, live in the Castro district and whenever I walk into their neighborhood I feel as if I am cutting on the bias through a spontaneous gay pride parade. It is a demonstrative locale to say the least, not unlike what a tourist sees when walking through Provincetown or Key West.

Here is the thing: I say nothing, not even privately to my family members. I make no judgments while my kids keep their mouths running, making negative judgments about *me*. This is an obvious reversal of our family trait, so why does no one see it happening but me?

"You are so much the old-fashioned father," Melissa accuses. "Cassandra must continuously roll her eyes."

"I am *not* one of those people that cause other people to roll their eyes. Just because I disapprove of your television station's championing these people every chance you get does not mean I am old-fashioned. Live and let live, I say."

" 'These people '? There you Go, Dad."

"Oh, stop it. I know what you … ah … media types say once the camera is turned off; you don't catch me doing the same. I know that you, and Jason, and Judy, and Martin Jr., too, not to mention your mom, *have* in fact made anti-gay cracks now and again. I heard you."

"Dad, you are the intolerant one by definition."

Right.

Christi is head of a child-protection unit in the city's social service system. She is one of those people who make decisions on whether or not children ought be removed from a home. She is mannish looking if I am allowed to say so objectively, though I do not hold that against her. I have no trouble gazing right into Christi's eyes though I will admit that her very faint, high-pitched, little girl voice does make me uncomfortable when it marches forth from that square-jawed face. Mixed signals do confuse me.

Christi is not a monster. The case is just the opposite. I like the woman. She is a *regular guy.* Jason yells at me when I say this but it is true; Christi is a regular fellow. She is a big time baseball fan and she and Cassandra have season's tickets to the San Francisco Giants games. Cassandra has to miss a lot of these games because of her priestly duties, so on more than one occasion Christi has called me up and asked me to go with her. They are good seats right behind first base. I have gone to a couple of games with Christi though I will say she never invites me when the Dodgers are in town.

But all this is by way of distraction. Christi and Cassandra love to obfuscate where I am concerned: they love these gender-bender situations and who better to trip up with the particulars than me? I have shared this with Judy by E-mail and she has this slant on it:

"Dad, they are playing a joke on you without even trying because you are such an easy mark. What you have to do is show some genuine magnanimity and your relationship with Cassandra will blossom."

"Cassandra and I get along famously."

"Oh, Dad, do we have to drag you kicking and screaming into the Twenty-first Century?"

Judy actually wrote that non-rejoinder during our last E-mail exchange. Yet I focus on it: again, and without stint, everyone insists that the problem with Cassandra resides with me but without admitting that there *is* a problem with Cassandra to begin with.

I say I am the only one who is being honest here. I am the silent liberal when it comes to gay rights; why does that make me the right-winger? It is wearisome, really, how this pattern of unfairness keeps repeating itself. My no good, soon to be ex-wife and my five children all *need* me around to be the designated whipping boy and frankly I do not like that role. Though whenever I try to articulate my position only one word forms on their lips:

"Curmudgeon."

I will press on objectively regardless. I ask: how is it that I am the only one in the family in constant contact with my daughter, Cassandra, while I am yet considered, in the eyes of the rest of our family, to be estranged from Cassandra? How is it that *I* am to blame for the unacknowledged yet alleged rift between us when, to be brutally realistic, Sophia, Jason, Judy, Melissa, and even Martin Jr., though they would rather cut off their tongues than admit it, are deep down in their souls more opposed to Cassandra's so-called marriage to Christi than I ever was or could be? *They* are politically liberal but privately sneaky; I am the upright guy. We never talk about that truth. Honestly, how I could it be that I am against my own daughter when I love and respect and *treat* all my offspring equally? I sigh. I am beating a dead horse.

All right, then, I will extend the principle of charity to my family. I will, voluntarily, go as deep as I can into me. I will try to analyze myself; I will try and fathom what my family is referring to when they point fingers at me. What is their intuition?

I never said this before but I do wonder where Cassandra got that *thick* body she has. It sure doesn't help that she still wears jeans coveralls now that she is all grown up, and it does not help that she covers herself up with flowing and billowing priest robes when she is working. It would be stupid of me to conclude that *if* there was any kind of real estrangement between Cassandra and me that it would have to do with her thick body, but I do not shrink from at least considering such a thing. How is that? How much more do you want from me?

Marty, I say to my self, be careful. You are just running your mouth now. Why is that? Do you *like* being labeled a curmudgeon by your family because you can then go to any length defending yourself while taking oblique jabs back at them?

As I have indicated earlier, I am not dramatizing all of my relationships with my family at once. If I did that, if I turned this into a stage play, I would have to go ahead and record all Jason's relationships with his family, and then, simultaneously, Judy's, and so forth, and God knows there are a plethora of neurotic interchanges going on between brothers and sisters, and kids and mom. No. I am doing this sequentially. For now I am exploring the phenomenology of Marty, the father, and Cassandra, the daughter. I am looking into the core of our father-daughter relationship.

What are the basics? I am the daddy. I am considered a bad daddy. I am considered a selfish man. That is what is behind the common family claim that I am not fully embracing Cassandra and her lifestyle while it is obvious that I do it better than the rest. What they are telling me, I think, is that my capacity for thinking logically has somehow failed me when it comes to loving: somehow I have squandered my intellectual gift by expending it in trivial pursuits while holding it back from what counts. Silent liberalism is the enemy my family wants to root out of my soul. *They* want to be totally independent of me while reserving the right to be aggrieved members of my family, too.

Here is the thing. If I were to upload these words and send them out to my wife and children they would all pounce at once. They would insist that I am losing it. They would insist that I am having a senior moment. I will grant them this much: I am not thinking logically at the moment. I admit it, but so what? I am a human being, too. I have to juggle sameness and difference, motion and rest within my humanness. I admit I can lose it on a given day. Yet the question remains: why does that make me churlish? Why does it indicate to them that I may be senile? It is because my family insists that I am not just another old man who does not know his place.

Put it this way. We all lived together as a family within sight of the V-J Grocery. I love going there. I went there with my kids as they were growing up. I went there with Sophia. I rubbed shoulders with my neighbors there. I still run into grey-haired Lois there, though I admit I am growing wary about Lois. So it was that everyone I know or knew observed me at V-J. They saw my impatience when standing in line to be served or to check out my purchases; they saw how I would grind my teeth when someone wasn't moving fast enough for me down an aisle. They can all trace my disagreeableness back to these experiences if they wish; that one example can stand in for the whole of my character.

Here it is, then. Everyone has the right to go down an aisle of a grocery store at his or her own reasonable pace. Yet *I* show impatience. I show people *up.* Extrapolating from that tiny sin, that little lack of graciousness, my family has decided that I am not fit to live in a city like San Francisco.

Is that true? If it is, then is that all there is to it? I am an impatient man. None of my kids took after me and my wife turned out to be an airhead. Now I am getting old and my kids have grown tired of me. My wife left me because she decided to make a change while she still has a vestige of her looks and most of her energy. Is that it? If that is it then why is it that Lois, who knows about my impatience in the grocery store, as do my kids, wants to get together with me? Well, in all honesty Lois hasn't *yet* said anything of the sort but I say that is only a matter of time.

Fourteen

My second son and youngest child, Martin Jr., was born in 1978 and celebrated his thirtieth birthday recently. Does that suffice?

OK. I will admit that I don't even know if I have the will to write about Martin Jr. after telling you about Jason, Judy, Melissa, and Cassandra, and this is true even if I hold onto my pattern and continue to separate the person from what he or she does in the world and thus stands for culturally. Martin Jr. always made me weary. Martin Jr. always made me sigh.

Instead of comparing Junior to me, I have always tended to compare him to my first born, Jason, and usually in the physical sense only. Jason is tall and athletic; Junior is short and reminds me, always, of the long-gone hippies. The fact that he is not a hippie doesn't matter: I think of him that way.

If Melissa grew up adopting girlish ways through some sort of electronic media osmosis, then Junior grew up *sympathizing* with the women's movement in somewhat the same manner. I just never got over that; it reminds me of the student who stood up in my class and declared that all women were victims of men. I did and I do treat Martin like I do all my children; I love him as much as any of the others. I am the liberal. Yet Junior wearies me. He always has. In fact, this is as much a commentary on the deterioration of the educational process going on today in academia as it is on Junior; logic having gone the way of Latin. But I do not want to digress.

When he was six years old I observed Junior walking home from school while crisscrossing Clay Street over and over again. I could not figure out what he was doing or why. When I asked him he said,

"Dad, I cross the street whenever a woman is coming towards me because I do not want to give offense."

This from the mouth of a six year old who had yet to come up to a full-grown woman's knee; obviously he had just memorized a chunk of ideological nonsense, which was understandable. The question was why *that* particular chunk of nonsense? I never found a satisfactory answer to my question but it did not matter, for Junior remained consistent; his entire ego development was centered around the women's movement and I confess this left me, his father, feeling like some sort of cliché macho guy with no place to flick his fat cigar ashes, or store the ammo for his shotgun. You know the image: an overweight slob who can't get his belt over his beer gut or who can't help telling out of date jokes about "the wife" to women who insist that men are pigs.

Of course everyone else in the family praised Junior and ganged up on me when I tried to instill a bit of pride in the kid regarding his own gender. Judy, whom I suspect was the one feeding the boy all these polemics, was especially strident.

"Dad, you should be proud of Junior. He is ahead of the curve. He sees how our culture is evolving. He embraces the revolution. You, on the other hand, being left behind in Junior's dust."

"That is so wrong, darling. I am all for gals getting what they want out of this world. I am. It is just that … ah … the *rhetoric* that goes with it makes me ill. Why can't Junior grow up to be a regular guy while you gals grow up to be regular girls who accomplish whatever you want and God bless you?"

"Oh, Dad, don't take all those provocative statements seriously. It is still a man's world."

"I wonder."

Anyway, Junior started growing up and soon enough he didn't need Judy to fight his battles for him. On the contrary, he began fighting battles for Judy and for all the other woman's causes one could think of; he came to their aid whether they asked him to or not. Junior told me early on, when he was a freshman in high school in fact, that he was going to devote his life to the women's movement and that he considered this to be equivalent to the Civil Right's movement of the 1960's. He and I disagreed totally on that subject.

"Junior, all these women are doing is stealing the thunder from the ongoing Civil Right's movement."

"No, Dad. Women are in step with black people. They are after the same freedoms."

I couldn't convince Junior he was wrong. I couldn't convince him that the day would come when women, white women that is, and blacks of both genders would clash openly over the shrinking supply of economic spoils there were to be had out in the world. Time would prove me right of course though Junior has never acknowledged that.

In any case I am getting ahead of myself; I want, as long as I have started in on Junior, to complete this sketch of his childhood.

I went to San Francisco Giant baseball games; Junior attended women's softball games. I offered my son private lessons in predicate logic; he preferred to read articles on sexual harassment. By the time he was a senior in high school Junior and I got into shouting matches at least once a week over his ready adoption of each and every new feminist polemic coming out, and at that time they were coming out as regularly as mosquitoes out of still water. I was especially hurt by this because I had, with Junior as with all my other children, established early on the distinction between rigorous philosophical argumentation and advocacy tactics. The thing was Junior *shamelessly* moved in the opposite direction, and consciously so.

"We *want* to promote false consciousness in the public, Dad. Don't you get it? This is the only way we will be able to move women forward. This is the only way to break their bounds."

Well, he had a point. *If* one was going to promote revolution then one could, taking Marx as one's guide, eschew the first form of the division of labor, sex, and free women and children from the slavery of the husband and father. Yet Jason went far, far beyond Marx. He, and his feminist colleagues, used *Lenin* and not Marx to push their agendas. That was like waving a red flag in front of me. Aside from their plagiarism, I had this complaint.

"Those tactics are …ah … unfair Junior; don't you admit to that? Why, in the end, you won't break down the family in favor of the state."

"Why not, Dad?"

"Because the bourgeoisie class will never waste away. What will happen is this. Eventually the majority of professionally educated women will marry educated men and in the last analysis they will join the ranks of the upper middle class and drive the opportunities and wages of the middle and lower middle class folk into such a depressed position that class warfare and the traditional family structure will be more entrenched than ever. Junior! You are simply waging war on poor women all over the world."

"I can't help that, Dad. I am committed to helping women break glass ceilings. Besides, the crap you are telling me is the same crap you are trying to feed Judy."

Fifteen

Junior went to San Francisco State. He wasn't much of a scholar; he spent most of his time running for various student offices, none of which he won by the way, in promoting women's causes, in bothering deans, and attending feminist conferences on the east coast at my expense, conferences at which he admitted that he was not given prominent roles but was used only as part of a marginal support team. As far as I understood it, Junior was kept around as the designate whipping boy, a position I could readily identify with myself.

I had no hopes for my son and my expectations for him were non-existent. Yet here is where he surprised me. Junior emerged a hard-driving strategist for a single woman's cause, that of getting more women into political office. He told me upon graduation from college,

"I figured it out, Dad. My running for office so as to promote women was chauvinism personified. I was in danger of being labeled paternalistic, which is the dirtiest of all labels."

"Thank you for that, Junior."

"What I ought do is help *women* run for office. That is my niche."

Junior went on to law school. Junior did well in law school. Junior came out of law school and has been hiring himself out as a strategist for democratic women candidates ever since. He is damn good at what he does. He makes a good living; he makes enough money to live well in this expensive city. He manages every facet of a political campaign. He would hate to have me say this but I will: he orders women about like a Nineteenth Century foreman would his female labor staff, except that he does it all for their own good as far as he envisions it. Thus it is that my son has demonstrated his masculinity after all while busily promoting his women's causes. This leaves me in another one of those quandaries: I both like and dislike what is happening with Junior, though, in any case, I remain the silent liberal.

Junior directs campaign financing for his hopefuls. He handles the media. Here he gets a great boost from Melissa, who manages to get a lot of stuff on the air gratis that would normally cost a candidate an arm and a leg. He handles voter registration, sets up rallies, writes speeches, what have you; Junior is a hands-on, micro-manager type who is a total stranger to me these days. I confess that while I am not all that excited about women in politics, I must admire my son's professionalism in landing them in office. This is not lost on Junior, who has taken to chiding me of late; my youngest son literally treads me like an old fuddy-duddy.

"How old are you now, Dad? Seventy five?"

"Seventy-two!"

"Really? You look older."

"Thank you."

"Come on, Dad. You are so out of it. The woman's movement has succeeded. Women are into every aspect of our society. Yet we need to see more numbers. We have overcome a good deal of nonsense and now it is time for the next cultural step."

"I suppose I am part of the overcome nonsense."

"And how! Dad? I know the rest of your children do call you a curmudgeon but I never got much into that. I just recognized you for what you were, a member of a soon to be extinct generation whose values were destined to be superseded. You have your gruff ways but I never considered the personal side of it. I framed you in terms of the women's movement exclusively. Dad? It is not that you are a disgruntled old man so much as it is that your male generation was misogynistic. It was engrained in all of you. So, go with the flow. Don't take any of this personally. You have been passed by."

"Ah, yes, my youngest child explains his father to his father using the same terminology, as did his siblings. But I wonder this: *is* the world better off now that women are flooding into politics, law, finance, and business? I ask you this while setting aside the still relevant facts to do with childrearing. Who is to say that women are going to do a better job than men? Who is to say that in the long, long run the women's movement will be good for the human race?"

Junior only laughed. Junior and I are not shouting at one another anymore. We discuss these issues, though we remain like two ships passing in the night. He does not convince me of his vision nor do I get him to take my counter-arguments seriously.

Most of all I don't even see the so-called gains women make *percentage wise* as being permanent. What I said to Jason when he was in high school still goes: the feminists helped an elite number of women and have abandoned the rest.

"Junior. Do me this favor. Go visit an eye doctor practice. What you will see is this. The entire out-on-the-floor staff, dressed in white, will be women; the half dozen eye doctors lurking in the back offices will be men. Women lawyers are only working part time for the most part; women have forged that compromise for themselves and don't bore me by telling me that men won't do half the housework. Every one of these women has their own housekeeper."

"Anything else, dad, while you are on a roll?"

"Tattoos!"

"What's that?"

"You were instrumental in telling girls they could do anything they wanted. Well, they listened to you. They went out and mutilated their bodies like a bunch of drunken sailors. They did not get the hidden message. Instead of their interpreting the idea that they can do anything they like to mean they ought break glass ceilings, they take it literally and go out and act crudely."

"Dad, I can live with that so long as we can push *some* women to the top. I mean it. Look at your own daughters. Judy is a smashing success. Melissa is a smashing success. Cassandra is a groundbreaker. Even Mom had the courage to …"

"Go ahead, say it."

"To escape from you, Dad."

"Was I that much of a tyrant?"

"You were."

This makes me laugh, but only to myself. Junior's control over his women candidates makes me blush.

When the baby of the family turns the tables on his father and starts offering radical hermeneutical descriptions of what went on in his household during his upbringing it is time for the father to let loose a mighty sigh. I *am* a true liberal. Junior will learn that the hard way one day.

What I am talking about is this. I knew plenty of so-called liberal politicians here in the city who, when the minorities they promoted started running for office on their own, turned on a dime and started spouting racist rants. Junior thinks he is above all that but I disagree: there will come a time when some of the very women he gets into office will dump him in favor of female campaign managers. Mark my words. Junior will have fits. He will argue that he is more competent than the women replacing him but that will fall on deaf ears; Junior will be cast aside. Then again I am, in saying this, aware as well that I foresee the day when women will start leaving the work force in significant numbers. That is a slip up. Then again, I could be very, very wrong. I really don't know my politics.

For that reason I must listen to myself more carefully; I must be ever vigilant nowadays. I am getting old after all. I have spent too much time listening to my own family members, so much so that of late I spend a part of every day worrying about my logical skills. I go into panics thinking that I will be transforming a verbal argument into logical symbols so as to check it for validity when, of a sudden, I won't be able to recognize the symbols themselves. Then my kids will gather together for a summit on what to do about the old geezer. I can just imagine!

"We can't leave Dad in that big apartment by himself. He will burn the place down. We have to get him in a home."

Who will lead the charge? Junior? Jason? Judy? Melissa? Cassandra? I'll bet it would be Sophia. I'll bet she wants nothing more than to come back to the west coast and live here in this place on what is left of my money.

Sixteen

Martin Junior lives on Greenwich Street on Russian Hill with his wife Tulip, whom he met in law school, and their two-year old daughter Hillary in a renovated rooming house they converted into a gracious one family home. In keeping with his principles my son chose to take his wife's last name instead of vice versa; he is now known around the city as Attorney Martin Zajac Jr. As for his retaining the junior moniker, don't even ask.

Tulip is a lobbyist for an environmental agency and spends most of her time down in Sacramento, where the Zajacs keep a condo, though she works out of this city, too. Junior works long hours at his office here in San Francisco and is out virtually every evening at candidate dinners or at other fundraisers, so a French nanny by the name of Selene looks after Hillary full time. Sophia used to help out with babysitting but now that she is gone off to South Beach in Miami Beach Selene does it all. I volunteered to baby sit when the girl was just a year old but Tulip and Junior politely, and I would add, somewhat frostily declined my offer. When I took offence Junior came to visit me on Nob Hill and, during a rambling, plenary, father-son session outlined several bogus reasons why he and Tulip did not find me suitable as a part time caretaker for my own granddaughter. I will try, just here, to re-enact just one of the highlights of Junior's negative assessments of me along with my own, admittedly feeble protest.

"Dad, you are incorrigible. You know that, don't you?"

"In what way?"

"Every time a child falls into your clutches you try to teach him or her logic, as if that was the key to eternal happiness, the ultimate knowledge of the universe, and … God help us … lots of fun. Dad, they have logic machines for that nowadays. Computer engineers are in charge of that stuff. Logic has a practical bent; kids don't want to learn it just to … Dad? You are so old fashioned that, I don't know, you are the only person I know who still works with paper and pen and …"

"I use a computer!"

"Dad, I was only exaggerating to make a point."

"You think I would ruin your child with my old ways?"

Junior declined to answer that one directly. Instead he referred, vaguely, to the bigger picture.

"Cultural losses happen. Hillary is going to get in on the new situation; her mother and I want her totally separated from the past."

"Your mother wasn't exactly…"

"I couldn't say no to Mom. With you it is different."

"You don't want your daughter to know about cultural history?"

"No, we really don't. We want her to grow up with a clean slate. We want her to forge ahead without pause, without emotional baggage of any sort. As for us, her parents, we would never want to be in the position where we would be tempted to complain that our daughter has forgotten or, worse, does not appreciate what sacrifices others have made for her. Hillary must have no impediments so that …"

"What are you saying, exactly, Junior?"

"Dad, Hillary is going to be the President of the United States one day. I hope to direct her campaign."

"You mean … your Hillary?"

"Yes."

"And she won't be without impediments if she hangs around with me?"

"Tulip and I feel that is the case."

That was hard, though Junior did add,

"You can still visit Hillary once a month so long as one of us, or both of us are there. There is no harm in that."

We silent liberals are not proud. I made the short walk from Nob Hill to Greenwich Street on the average of one weekend evening a month for dinner over this past year, though it was not uncommon for Junior, and for Tulip, too, to be called away during the fish course to attend some hastily called meeting. When that happened the nanny, Selene, was brought into the room from wherever they stored her and, with this new trio composed of Granddad, Granddaughter, and Frenchwoman at the table, the atmosphere changed radically.

"More roast beef, Professor Parrish?"

"You are too kind, Selene. Yes I will have another helping. And I will pour you another glass of this excellent red wine."

"Oh, la-la."

On those rare nights, when the parents were still out stomping for female political candidates who would secure the future of the environment, and little Hillary had been put to bed, I entertained Selene with tales of this town going back to the Nineteenth Century. I figured that if Hillary were not going to have history in her life it would mean all the more for this Frenchy.

Selene is thirty-six. She is tall, not *too* fleshy, and quite fetching in a European sort of way. She has Sundays off unless the Zajacs are out of town and, after turning down four invitations by batting her long light brown eyebrows to show her Continental modesty she finally consented to visit me here on Nob Hill. One thing led to another and, needless to say the *situation* at this very moment has become explosive.

To get to the point: a few days ago my no good, soon to be ex-wife Sophia found out that Selene and I plan a wedding as soon as my divorce is through and all hell has broken loose. I am not sure how she found out but I have my suspicions. Whenever I walk over to V-J Grocery these days the grey-haired widow Lois gives me the evil eye. I suppose hell hast no fury like a woman who assumes she was scorned when she was not ever in the running. I never promised Lois anything and I cannot worry about her now.

Bottom line is Sophia dropped everything and is at this very moment airborne. Before she left for the west coast she called all five of our children and told them she was halting her divorce proceedings. Of course the kids are furious; every one of them took their mother's side and for the past twenty-four hours I have been inundated with visits, phone calls, and E-mails all telling me that in addition to being a damn curmudgeon, a chauvinist, a misogynist, and a dinosaur, I am now an old fool as well.

In fact Jason just left the apartment after yelling at me and, as he went out the door, slamming it, he had a few choice words in French for Selene who, I must say, is showing remarkable bravery.

"Dad! What the hell are you thinking? This … *cocotte* is just using you. She will marry you only to gain permanent residence in the United States and once she has that she will dump you in a nanosecond and grab our family home here in Nob Hill."

Melissa called while the door was still reverberating and started screaming in my ear.

"Dad! Dad! You are seventy-two. That woman is thirty-six. Do you know what that means?"

"I guess it means Selene is exactly half my age."

"Dad!"

Sophia's plane will be landing in an hour. On top of everything else memories of my wife and of our life together are flooding into my consciousness and I am unable to suppress them. I feel like one of those people whose life starts flashing in front of their eyes while their automobile is careening off a cliff. Only in my case the chosen loop is a bit more selective.

Seventeen

I was an unabashed Young Turk when I began teaching logic at San Francisco State. I insisted students drop everything else in their lives, be it personal or academic, and do nothing but logic problems. I would so terrify my charges with the prospect of flunking my course they would end up not studying for their other courses and, for the sake of satisfying my requirement, inevitably did poorly in every other subject.

"Makes no difference," I would counter in a stern voice. "Your mind will be disciplined. New pathways will be forged in your brain. You will know what it means to ride above the fray. You will see clearly."

Members of my own department suggested I ease up on students who were just passing through but I rejected their advice. I suppose I reveled in the idea that I was the most feared assistant professor on campus and, wouldn't you know, lots of students took up my challenge. The rumor went around that if one could crack Parrish's course one would get on in life.

I admit that not one of the students who ever passed through my course ever went on to become a professional logician, but that is OK; I know their lives are better for having been properly organized. At least I think as much, though no one ever wrote me a letter saying so.

I held philosophy majors up to a much higher standard. I made them into logic machines. This was fascinating. Students with no logical or mathematical bent were required to sit at their desks up to six hours a day doing logic problems and, here is the best part, not only did I make them keep this up until they *were* machine-like, I still would not let them go until they were so further conditioned they voluntarily came to me to thank me for the rigorous program I was submitting them to.

I was just a teacher nonetheless. My articles got me tenure, and eventually a full professorship, and nothing else: I never cracked the big time. How many people do? I was content in being known as the crusty academic, allowing that the university system was bigger than I was.

Nevertheless there were problems regarding my relationship with students. Students would complain that if I was not famous, like Aristotle, or Russell, or Frege, then why was I justified in being so ferocious on a single Californian campus? What could I say? I went from being known as a Young Turk to being known as a kind of academic curmudgeon. The years just passed in that manner.

But my thoughts now take me back to the beginning. One Monday in September during my second year of teaching I began an intro philosophy class by handing out baby logic assignments. I should explain that I routinely ignored what was expected of me in these introductory level courses, or in any other courses for that matter, and bent everything in a logical direction; I know how to teach every conceivable kind of philosophy by straining it through the methodology of logic and who was to stop me?

As I was passing out the sheets a student named Sophia Hardcastle caught my eye. Sophia was attractive enough. She *looked* intelligent, and when I went out of my way to speak to her, an honor in itself, she broke out into freshman-level blushes and giggles. Without hesitation I said, right there in the class,

"Come to my office tomorrow and pick up a special assignment. That is an order."

She came to my office.

I wasted no time; I told her that logic was life. Sophia had no idea what I was talking about but in her limited experience I was obviously someone of vast importance.

Over the next couple of weeks I had her return to my office on a daily basis, telling her that private tutorials in logic were the only way a student could get ahead, the only way a student could rise up out of the mass classroom milieu and not get lost in the shuffle, adding that I considered her a candidate for such privileged lessons.

"Thank you, Professor Parrish."

"Sophia?"

"Yes, sir?"

"When we are alone in my office you call me Marty."

I was undergoing a good deal of upheaval in my life at the time; both my parents were suffering terminal illnesses and my sister on the east coast was leaving all the family responsibilities to me.

What happened next surprises me even now. I told Sophia one day that in order for her to be fully developed as a person she would have to submit to an older dominant male who knew what was best for her, and she did. She dropped out of college, married me, and came to live with me on Nob Hill. Her family had their reservations but I handled that most adroitly; I assured them that once their daughter was privately trained in clear and systematic thinking that she could return to school filled with priceless advantages.

They bought it, sort of. It helped that they were lower-middle class folk who were duly impressed with my apartment on Nob Hill. The fact that their daughter Sophia never did return to school is, I would argue in retrospect, beside the point; she never really had the mind for systematic thinking anyway, something we both came to the painful discovery of when our nightly logic sessions disintegrated into shameful, drag out fights; Sophia started crying and I started yelling; her transition from late adolescence into a famous adult logician was never going to happen.

We had lots of good sex instead. Three years of it by my count.

Now I know this sounds narrow and crude, simply awful if you will, but I have already indicated that Sophia is on her way here and my involuntary memories are flashing by fast. I am, against my own will, focusing on what others always, and I think unfairly, considered my mean nature, while the whole truth is that I managed to have a proper, conventional life despite what others would, and again unfairly, consider my character flaws.

Sophia and I *were* happy. True, my young wife did have *some* tendencies to go ahead and explore this world on her own but let's face it; she would have made a mess of it. I told her so in so many wise words.

"Darling, you are made for childbearing. You are made to be a mother. That is your calling. That is what you must do in this life. Anything else will spell unhappiness for you. I speak not for myself but only for you."

Sophia resisted as best she could, which was feebly, and after the three years of sexual if not marital bliss I just spoke of, her identity crisis was over as far as I could tell. She got pregnant with our first child. Jason was a big baby and Sophia had a good deal of trouble delivering him. The others gave her no such problems. She and I raised our family on Nob Hill and as far as I am concerned we did a darn good job of it. I should add that my in-laws never gave me any further trouble once Sophia was settled into her proper role and it helped that they moved back to Cleveland soon after Jason was born.

Eighteen

Accounting for the authenticity of Sophia's life under my enlightened guidance starting from the birth of our first born, Jason, when she was twenty two, to that time of her second identity crisis at the age of fifty-eight when by giving herself over to an absurd and futile gesture she bolted for Florida to practice not knowing what she was doing as a real estate agent trying to sell to unsuspecting Europeans second-rate hotel rooms partitioned off into partial ownerships is not an easy task under these hurried and compressed circumstances but I will give it a try.

Who says that Marx had it right? Who says that just because he *wrote* that sex makes mothers and children into the slaves of the husband and father that such an assertion is true?

Sophia couldn't stand up to logical training, so the next best thing she could do was give me children. That *they* were uniformly recalcitrant is another story, one I feel I have well documented, and in systematic fashion, above.

What I need do here is say *what* Sophia was about during her authentic years for, after all, a woman cannot *be* a mother twenty-four hours day, she has to live and breathe and waste her time doing something else on a daily basis.

She was a shopper.

Sophia shopped for shoes, for dresses, for curtains, for bras, for salt shakers, for silk flowers, for hand lotions, for heavy sweaters just in case we took a vacation in Alaska, for birthday presents, for picture frames, for warm socks for me, for the kids, for a rainy day, whatever. I would complain and be told to shut up; I would get mad and be ignored; I would show my wife the bills and be told that I was a typical husband who had nothing better to do but go on and on about his wife. All that was true but the thing was this was what made Sophia *tick.* She never, ever, once looked up into the foggy skies over San Francisco and shouted,

"Gee! What does it all mean? What is the meaning of life? Why am I here? Is there anything behind those grey clouds? When you set a bucket of water spinning while suspended from a rope, does the water rise up the sides of the bucket because of local centrifugal forces or because of universal gravitational forces, etc."

Well. OK. I am a bit cynical. So what? My wife did her motherly duty, her wifely duty, and her housewifely duties it is true. That is all I expected of her once I found out she couldn't or wouldn't do logic problems. Yet was it unreasonable of me to ask more? Was it unreasonable of me to want both to direct Sophia's life and to see her stand on her own two philosophically inquiring feet, too?

Now and again she would really, really frustrate me by getting into some pseudo study thinking she was now competing with me intellectually. She learned about wine tasting for instance. Good Lord! She would go off to Napa on bus tours, coming back home to bore me to tears with the jargon they filled her ears with, just so she could have sway at the dinner table. One time she got into Tarot card reading and went so far as to claim that there was a deep, *logical* basis to the scam. Another time she took up guitar lessons. Sophia has ten left thumbs. I let her plunk those strings for a year and a half but when she tried adding singing lessons I put my foot down; no wife of mine was going to embarrass me by showing up at some club on amateur night and making a fool of herself.

She did other stuff. She collected recipes, she collected movies, she collected glass figurines, she collected fat lumps of art pottery with the idea in mind to become an antique dealer though she never followed through, and she collected copies of the San Francisco Chronicle thinking that this pile of yellowing paper, this fire hazard, this home for bugs, this clutter, this closet-filling mess would be worth something one day. I tore my hair out over this one and thank God the kids backed me here: they were all worried that their mom was going to start out as a pack rat and end up in a loony bin. That little venture of hers ended one fine day when Jason and Martin Jr. took it upon themselves to toss the whole pile of newspapers out while their mom was off to Fisherman's Wharf buying more junk. When she got home she cried her eyes out but she knew it had to be.

Sophia took up volunteer work for a time. I would have been happier had she taken up a half way decent paying job instead but the ladies in the neighborhood had convinced her that she was some sort of society person and that she ought to act the part. Society person? I had to remind Sophia that she was from a blue-collar family from Cleveland who never made it in this town and for reasons obvious to one and all. My kids told me I was cruel to say this to their mom but I was not thrilled about all this volunteer stuff and didn't like the idea of my wife being out of the house when I expected my dinner. Sophia "got over" my being cruel to her regarding her humble background and she did become hoity-toity for a time, she sat on gala committees for arts festivals that went bankrupt, she licked stamps and envelopes for the San Francisco Opera, she rode the ferry back and forth to Sausalito promoting tourist rip offs, something she *ought* to have gotten paid to do but did not, and she served as a guide to the Moscone Convention Center, a task that gave her varicose veins.

Mostly, Sophia tried to come to life through our kids. Her efforts were met with resistance, though today the kids make use of selected memory to put the blame on me for the way they treated their mom. Once again, the old circular argument got put to use; dad was the designated fall guy by definition and that question-begging device is still in use up to the moment.

Jason was always good to his mother though he kept her at arm's length while growing up; tacitly agreeing with me that Sophia was not all that bright. I think Jason worried that his mother might jinx his chances of making use of his Ivy League education, though he would never say so. Suffice to know that he and I shared many a joke at Sophia's expense and that he wasn't above baiting her so that she was made the butt of his intellectual intrigues. When Jason launched his maddening franchise schemes Sophia tried to help out but Jason was wary; the best he could do was offer her the chance to work a cash register in one of his hardware stores. I read him the riot act for that.

When Judy grew up she kept Sophia at bay as well. Judy thinks her mom should have stood up to me decades ago and, since she did not, Judy further thinks this gives her the right to blame both of us for the way her parent's marriage turned out. I especially hate my daughter's take on the matter.

"Judy! All Sophia's disasters in life came when she stood up to me. And I resent the words "stood up to me" as well. I knew what was best for Sophia and besides, her only happiness in life came when she did in fact do what I thought best."

"Dad, you dominated your wife like one would a lap dog. You were a regular monster."

I wouldn't even grace that marginally mixed metaphor with a response.

Melissa provided the greatest opportunity for Sophia to have a *pal,* or to relive her life through, though, and as I indicated above, they were not quite a mother-daughter fit. I think it came down to the fact that while Melissa managed to transform her classic feminine nature into a professional job that pays for every trivial fact that is broadcast, Sophia just frittered her tendencies away on non-paying trivialities. They are close, Melissa and Sophia, though I suspect Sophia is driven by jealousy as far as our middle child goes.

Cassandra presented Sophia with her greatest challenge. I am a liberal, while Sophia is a closet gay-basher if you will permit me that expression. She never did come to grips with Cassandra's telling her mom she was a lesbian. Of course the whole business got conveniently turned around so that it is my fault not only for how Cassandra turned out but for holding it against her; once again the official story is that everyone in the family is OK with Cassandra but Daddy, while the truth is quite the opposite. But I am repeating myself.

Martin Jr. is a hard case. By the time he came along Sophia had become understandably weary doing my bidding for her own good. I say that to show some insight into my wife's psyche and to express some sympathy for her fate; I am not an ogre after all. I am merely a curmudgeon. I am not even a curmudgeon but I will graciously accept that false tag in lieu of being known as an evil person.

Martin Jr. made Sophia uneasy. His constant drumming for women's rights, his cheering on women trying to break glass ceilings, his political savvy, his insistence on turning women into aggressive fighters, left his mom with so many conflicting messages I swear there were times when Sophia was ready to drop her faux liberal stance and declare herself a rock rib conservative. Sophia said she wanted to be her own woman, yet she could only sleep at night when reassured that she was fulfilling all her duties as wife and mother. I can attest to that.

Martin Jr. never took the time to deal with his mother in a nuanced way that would reassure her that she was genuine while at the same time he was directing a brand new cultural wave that excluded Sophia. Martin left that task to me. That I failed to pick up the ball and play by his rules I blame on the fact that I, too, struggled with conflicts; I was doing what I thought best for my wife while observing my children forge new realities for themselves. It is one thing to take the simple out the way my kids did by labeling me a dinosaur; it was something else to implicitly drag their mother into the same depreciatory category.

Sophia and I were happy and we loved one another. We really did. It is just that I had what you might call this Pygmalion complex and, as fate would have it, it turned out that the joke was on me all the time. I loved a woman whose mind was neither logical nor deep. When I discovered that, *after* we were married, I continued to love her though she made it difficult for me to do so. It wasn't as if I had deliberately set out to marry a dumb wife just so I would have a faithful little lady waiting for me at home every night and to serve me my dinner, hand me my slippers and newspaper, and then sit at my feet looking up at me with rapt attention, batting her eyelashes and agreeing with whatever opinions I happened to spout without understanding what I was saying; on the contrary I remained faithful to my principles while it was Sophia who proved herself unable to develop logically. I continued to love her regardless of her shortcomings.

Thinking this over now, I must sigh. Sophia's leaving me and running off to Florida; to that falsely-hyped, mosquito-infested, boringly flat, insufferably humid, absurdly overcrowded cultural wasteland filled with alligators, snakes, rednecks, Disney characters, and swamp creatures was a terrible mistake on her part; she was no more equipped to stand on her own down there than would an aging family pet who never got out of the house except while locked in a carrying cage on the way to see the vet would have fared had it got separated from its master and gone wandering down Grant Avenue when all the restaurants were opening.

Nineteen

Sophia and I visited Miami Beach where I attended a logic conference as an emeritus professor. I was tied up all day for four days in a row while my wife spent her time walking up and down the boardwalk where she contracted a painful sunburn and marveled at all the high rise buildings jammed up against one another along the coastline. Evenings, my colleagues and I mingled poolside at our hotel stuffing our faces with the sorts of food offerings one wouldn't be caught dead ordering in sophisticated San Francisco and talking more logic. Our spouses were bored to the point of madness of course, but then again they were expected to be bored; they were the ones who could not or would not submit to systematic thinking.

I thought it might amuse Sophia to see how the masses of humanity waste their lives chasing shallow, pop culture values, so I took her down to South Beach on our final night in Florida where we made our way through that ever-present mob of thrill seekers while suffering the constant throb of awful music pounding in our ears and having to look at people who, after finally gaining an outside table at one of those overpriced cafes, were staring wide-eyed at passers by and assuring themselves they were in on "the scene". More than once I gave a depreciatory chuckle, turned to my wife, and asked,

"Have you ever experienced anything so completely crass in your entire life?"

Sophia said nothing.

We returned home to Nob Hill and I forgot all about hideous South Beach. Sophia had to see a doctor about her sunburn, but other than that I assumed that she put that bad trip out of her mind as well. I did fire off E-mail to the organizers of the logic conference, complaining about their choice of the host city. I told them that we had better get back to Helsinki and to a setting with more proper decorum.

Then, about a month later, all hell broke loose at our house.

I had been out all day searching through the independent bookstores in Haight Ashbury looking for rare editions of leftist polemics from the Nineteenth Century. I had been asked to give a talk at Berkeley and I wanted to provoke the audience with my knowledge of certain positions they took for granted. This way I could slam them with counter-arguments that would leave them gasping and then follow that up with my claim that I was the true liberal. Anyway, I got home about six that evening and there was Sophia standing in the doorway with three suitcases lined up at her feet.

"What is this now, darling? What do you think you are doing?"

"Marty. I am leaving you."

"Leaving me for what? Where are you going?"

"I am moving to Miami Beach to sell real estate."

"Sophia, you don't even have a salesman's license."

"I will get one."

I refused to fall for this dumb gambit from my wife. I went by her and into the house, casually speaking over my shoulder as I went.

"When you come to your senses get back in the house and cook dinner."

I was in the bathroom when the taxi came. Sophia went away.

She was on the phone two days later from Miami Beach asking for money. I sent it. I certainly thought it unwise to send Sophia money and thus feed her delusion, but I feared the reactions of my children. They all took their mother's side of course. Jason, speaking for his siblings, said, during one typical phone call,

"Dad! Mom has finally found the courage to strike out on her own. We applaud her. For too long she has been nothing but your doormat. She needs to have a life.

"Selling real estate down there is no life."

"Makes no difference, Dad. She needs to do it."

"She will fail."

"Again, it makes no difference."

I disagreed. I thought it made all the difference, though my children refused to listen.

As the weeks passed Sophia called again and again asking for money. Finally I flew down to see her. She was living in one room in one of those sad, old, paint-flaking, concrete squares at the far end of the strip, one of those buildings laughingly referred to as an "authentic example of art deco architecture". They had to be kidding. These decrepit buildings were nothing but square lumps of cheap construction upon which the builders had stuck one or two extraneous cement blobs, painted them blue or red, and called them fashionable. I said as much to my wife, who was again suffering sunburn, but she fired back with vehemence.

"These buildings are being rehabbed and each unit will sell for nothing less than half a million dollars."

I became calm. I became cool. I reminded Sophia of the real estate ventures going on in San Francisco, how so much money was being spent on rehabbing inferior construction there, and how, when one compared profits in that business against other investments, that there were far, far more losers than winners.

"Sophia, darling. The curve has curved. The mania is past. The suckers have been taken. The obscene profits have been made. The time for jumping into real estate sales in Miami Beach is long, long over. If you were destined to make money doing this sort of thing you would have started five or even ten years ago. You did not. Do you know why you did not? Darling, you hadn't a clue. You knew nothing about economic trends. You still haven't a clue. You are like one of those miner, forty-niners who came out to California in fifty-nine. The gold was all gone by then. All gone. Sophia, come home where you belong. I could, ah … we can begin all over again. We can still train your mind. Logic is …"

Sophia broke down crying. I tried to take her in my arms but she wouldn't let me. She was going to go ahead with this foolishness and that was that.

I made five more trips to Miami Beach this year. I financed my wife's entry into the business. I paid her rent and gave her expense money while she obtained her real estate selling license and went to work for a South Beach firm as a freelancer. They paid her not a dime; the idea is for her to sell units and gain some her commission from that.

While I was down there on my visits I took the trouble to look into what I already knew was the case. I likened it to a man who goes into his kitchen and counts two cups and two saucers and then double checks to make sure there are four entities counted.

"Sophia, it is *over*. The saturation point has been reached. There are no more sales to be made except to fools and if you manage to fool a fool then you are exposing yourself to ethical questions. All over the country the housing market is collapsing. The sub-prime mortgage scandal has struck. Do you read the papers anymore, or are you still stuck on the New York Times Style section? These so-called conversions whereby you push a windowless room at the back end of a failing hotel to a starry-eyed client who thinks he or she is "where it is at" while the hotel owners retain control of the whole building and dump excessive costs on the room buyer is … disgusting! What the hell are they mortgaging their futures for anyway? This is no place to live! It is too damn hot here! Look at you, Sophia! You are as red as a lobster and you are alternately sweating in the open air and shivering in the air conditioning, and for what? Do you read anything? The tax situation in this state is a scandal! It is a scam. You must have been told that the taxes go up when the sales prices rise. The big cheats have already fled, Sophia. If there really is anything of value left to sell in this place, do you seriously think they will let you sell it? Come home to San Francisco, darling. Come home to where you belong."

Sophia didn't cry this time. She *assumed* she was standing up to me when she shouted,

"Everyone has a right to stand on his or her own two feet and make a living. *You* made a living pushing symbols."

"Well, yes. I did. I did a good job of it in case you didn't notice."

Sophia's laughter was so sarcastic I was rendered mute. I had never heard that level of derision coming from the mouth of the woman I loved.

"Marty, you had our house handed to you gratis by your parents. You never had to *compete* in a real estate market that was spiraling upward; you just came home to Nob Hill every day. It turned you into a snob. But you didn't know enough to stop there. You insisted on torturing all of us with your 'if p then q' nonsense. You tell me I am wasting my time trying to sell condos, Marty. Can't you see that you wasted your whole life being a stubborn, opinionated, mean-spirited little tyrant?"

Twenty

Did you ever watch one of those delightful comedy movies where a skilled director places a stationary camera at one end of a corridor while the actors move in and out of doorways, dashing, or even strolling back and forth across the hall while failing to catch sight of one another or be caught out by one another by split seconds? Every character has an agenda plus something to hide, and every character may or may not be fully dressed. To the delight of the viewer these quick takes by an ensemble cast render the farce more complex, allude to off-screen sexual romps, and show various interlopers being absurdly intrusive, lucky, or madcap. The cast usually includes a wife, a mistress, a nosy neighbor, and several self-appointed moralists who may or may not be relatives of the principles but who inevitably feel they have the right to have their say.

Welcome to Nob Hill.

I didn't pick Sophia up at the airport because I was too busy scribbling and reassuring Selene that all would be well. Jason and Sally did the honors. Judy flew in from Europe after getting several frantic phone calls and Melissa and Mitch picked her up; Cassandra, Christi, Martin Jr., and Tulip arrived from their homes just as the others were getting here. My grandkids Michael and Susan were in tow, as well as baby Hillary; the youngsters were pretty much behaved except for Hillary, who kept crying out, "Selene! Selene!" It is the only word the kid knows.

Meantime Lois invited herself over on the pretence that she wanted to see Sophia again and so, with everyone even remotely connected to my misery being accounted for, the fun began.

I tried playing the father but to no avail. My kids told me to shut up, that it was all my fault, that I was a disgrace, that they would see to it that I was committed, that things had to stop right now, that I was killing Mom, and that they were tired of looking out for me. This last complaint escaped me completely.

I tried playing the husband but to no avail. Sophia was talking about divorce one minute, and about never letting me out of her sight again the next minute. Suddenly she seemed every bit as interested in our Nob Hill house as she did me, but without as much confusion showing or contractions stated.

"I'll never let you sell it, Marty, you sneaky bastard."

"I have no intention of selling it!"

"Living here in sin the way you are it ... it comes to the same thing!"

I tried playing the lover but to no avail. Selene was not as rattled as I thought she'd be, which upset me a little, but she was still upset, which upset me further. Then, starting the moment my family members showed up, she began noticing that I was twice her age *in earnest.*

"Will you be having a heart attack, Cheri?"

This was one man's family though I must confess my family in Nob Hill had little in common with Henry Barbour's fictional family, *One Man's Family,* coming to me as a child over the radio from Sea Cliff. My family soap opera was far more absurd.

Once she got here Sophia did not know where she ought sleep. She finally settled for our master bedroom, meaning that Selene and I had to abandon it. Not that Selene followed me into a guest room; she did not. She went down the hall to grab a room for her self only to be kicked out of that one minutes later by my irate daughter, Judy, who rightly laid claim to her childhood bedroom.

I got the idea of there being a light-touch movie director calling the shots at my place from watching Selene and Sophia running in an out of rooms managing to avoid direct contact with one another like matter and anti-matter. Selene did suffer the wrath of Martin Jr. and Tulip, who chased her into a bathroom calling her a home breaker. Selene stared them down bravely from behind a translucent shower curtain, gently reminding them they owed her, their former nanny, a paycheck and a half.

Melissa and Mitch played their usual roles as the shiny-tooth lightweights; they threatened to make me tomorrow's gossip on local television and I told them to go right ahead and try it. They immediately backed off.

Jason and Sally were furious with me, insinuating that their children were being corrupted by the reckless behavior of their grandfather and I admit this did seem likely; Michael and Susan ran around the house like a couple of ferrets let loose, and at one point began chanting in singsong,

"Granddad's got a girl friend. Granddad's got a girl friend."

Meanwhile Cassandra pulled a priest move; she plopped down on her fat knees right in the middle of the living room and began praying for all of us in an ear-piercing singsong voice. That checked our activities for a moment or two, or only until Christi sidled over to my wife and, in a faux whisper one could hear out on Clay Street, volunteered to beat Selene to within an inch of her life. Sophia didn't seriously consider the offer, though she did hesitate for a second or two.

In the midst of the hubbub Tulip had the bright idea to call for Chinese food and while we were all at the dining table digging into our boxes I swear I saw Mitch making what I thought was a pass at Selene by cleverly dropping some pork fried rice off the ends of his chop sticks onto her lap and then deftly retrieving each grain with little scissor like snaps. Before I could say anything Hillary approached her nanny once again and, while Selene was downing mouthfuls of lamb two styles the child gave Frenchy a hug. Selene was kind enough to reciprocate though even I could see the wheels of her mind turning as she did so; no doubt she was asking herself if it was all worth it just to stay in this country and in this city where there were so many hills and so much fog.

Martin Jr. bored everyone at this point by going out of his way to make some gratuitous and totally disparaging remarks about women who take low jobs, and Tulip followed this by adding further cracks about Selene's perfume, which even I have to admit she wears too much of, at least by foggy, hilly west coast standards.

Worst of all was grey-haired Lois. She couldn't make up her mind just who to direct her insults to for the longest while, turning her evil eye from me, to Selene, and even to Sophia in that order, while shuffling white rice into her mouth. She wouldn't take a hint to leave the table let alone the house, nor would she take a direct order from Judy.

"Get the hell out of here you old meddling hag."

Finally Lois leaned over to me and spit out,

"You could have had a real Nob Hill woman. I would have been cheaper by far and a better investment, too. We could have pooled our real estate."

Jason had heard enough. He pounded the table with his big fist and Lois finally left us but not before grabbing the leg of a Peking duck and marching out the door with it. The rest of us went on chewing. Once the Chinese food was finished and cleared off the table Judy, my high-powered European-marketing-queen daughter, the only one of us who seemed to be clinging to anything like a professional presence, offered to broker a solution that, when we all heard it coming out of her mouth, made no sense to anyone but Selene. The reason for that was simple: Judy spoke French.

She spoke in French for ten straight minutes while Selene sat in rapt attention and while the rest of us sat there fidgeting and pulling long faces. The next thing I knew Selene got up and made her way down the hallway towards the bedrooms without even a backwards glance at me. I turned to Judy.

"What did you say to that poor young woman?'

The rest of the family members were just as curious as I was and so held their tongues. It was as if we were suspects in a criminal investigation and Miss Marple was now going to name the culprit. Of course, that culprit would have to be me, and by definition, though I let Judy speak her mind regardless.

"Dad, I told Selene that if she returns to Europe without causing any more disruption I would hire her as a personal assistant where I work. She was dubious of my offer at first but when I threw out a starting salary she jumped at it. I promised her a signing bonus as well."

"Then where? What is she doing now?"

"She is packing."

"What about her promising to marry me?"

"Come on, Dad. Wise up. Be *logical.* All I had to do was wave the promise of serious money under that girl's nose and she gave you up on the spot. I would imagine her having to marry you in order to get somewhere would have been like submitting to an outbreak of hives. Don't you think?"

I had no comeback. I had no counter-argument. I was chagrinned. Judy stared me down and then turned to Sophia.

"Mom? Dad is right about one thing. South Beach is tapped out. You will never make a dime there. Besides, your children and grandchildren want you to come home where you belong."

Sophia, who was close to shedding tears of relief if not joy, protested feebly. "But your father will start in on me all over again. He won't let me work and—"

"Yes, he will. Mom, you can start slowly and sensibly this time. Get yourself a California real estate license and start selling homes here. This market will never slow down. And who knows the market here in San Francisco better than you?"

Sophia was shedding buckets of tears now and the kids were grinning and soon enough all eyes turned to me as if to say "don't screw it up this time you old fart."

I did not screw it up, except for one minor lapse in judgment when I offered to drive Selene to the airport.

Suffice to say we have come to a semi-happy ending here on Nob Hill. We have compromised. I am allowed to walk around grousing about anything and everything I wish these days with one stipulation: neither Sophia, nor our kids, nor our grandkids for that manner, pay me any attention whatsoever. I still think that if everyone would just take the time to think systematically we would all be better off though I know it will never happen. Logician-kings are too good for this world, which is a damn shame.

Avon CT, July 2008